VOMA Publications

https://www.authorjbrinkley.com/

Cover Design: Amb Branding (Aija Monique)

Editor: Monica Walters

https://www.authormonicawalters.com/

TABLE OF CONTENTS

Chapter One

Police sirens blared against the loud bass of rap music, drowning out Brecee's jagged breathing. Sweat poured down the side of his face as his hands gripped onto the steering wheel hard enough to irritate his callouses.

It was another close night where his lazy customers were sloppy as usual.

"Fucking college kids," he mumbled in between catching his breath. His heart was pounding like crazy in his chest as he listed off every reason jail would ruin him.

Aside from his dad having a messy record, it was the last thing he needed to put on his mother's plate.

He swerved the car wildly into a hidden passage and sped through the dark woods. His eyes were wide with fear as the ecstasy of, yet again, another police car made his pulse skyrocket into oblivion.

"They can't fucking get me. They can't fucking get me," Brecee chanted as he continued to dash through the woods. He dodged broken branches that hung in wiry clusters. Some swiped the hood of his busted cars and others skirted over the hood.

His eyes danced from his rearview mirror to the dark, uncharted woods before him. There was a buzzing to his left that alerted him of another distraction.

"Not now," Brecee said through gritted teeth. He finally made it to a clearing and stopped the car, turning it off to listen.

The police sirens were barely present. He could hear them blaring in the opposite direction, taking them far away from him.

Brecee sighed and grabbed his phone, reluctantly redialing the missed call. It rang three times before a frantic Zach answered.

"Nigga, what the hell was that? Zee is gonna murder us," he barked on the other line. Brecee inhaled sharply through his nose to keep his emotions in check. Unexpected plans were always sure to ruffle dealers, but if you lost your cool it'd be a done deal.

"Lil nigga tried to play with me and have his boys pull a gun out," Brecee explained flatly. Brecee and Zach only worked together twice, but Brecee could already tell Zach only had two more chances before he got caught up.

Zach's breathing became more jagged as fear leaked out into his tone.

2

"Did you kill them?" he screeched. Brecee held his phone down, disgusted by Zach's lack of solid thinking.

Does this dude think I'm stupid?

"Obviously, I'm not that impulsive," he replied slowly. "Just meet me at the clearing off of that neighborhood's road."

"Aight, man."

Brecee threw his phone across the seat as frustrated tears spilled down his cheeks. The moon was right above his car and shone through his window, blinding him.

The streets were getting more and more ruthless and Brecee knew it was only a matter of time before he ended up exactly like his father.

"You must wanna end up in that prison right next to your damn daddy," his mother had yelled at him the last time she spoke to him. He had just escaped another cop chase after a bad deal. It wasn't that he didn't know how be discreet, but he was young. Most folks that saw him just saw a baby-faced kid who they could easily overpower.

He wasn't a pushover, though.

The night was finally quiet again with the faint hum of crickets and the distant soundtrack of the city life. Brecee sat back and closed his eyes, basking in the coolness of the night sky. His thoughts slowed down and he imagined he was back in the city as a kid, holding tight onto his parents' hands.

It was just months before his dad would be arrested and thrown into prison, but in that moment things were blissful. Brecee was small and protected underneath the shadows of his parents. The streets were littered with smiling faces lost in their conversations, and the sky was sticky and sweet with hotdogs and funnel cakes.

Brecee had reached out for it and could feel the hot sun eating away at his skin. It sizzled and melted his ice cream, but the heat felt joyful especially when he was wedged between his mother and father. When he looked up, they were beaming at one another as if they were one of those couples in picture frames.

We fit, we finally fit, the eight-year-old Brecee had thought.

There was a rustle of bushes and Brecee's eyes shot open, the dream quickly dissipating. He put his hand on his gun and slowly eased the car door open. His heart was racing as usual, but he kept his jaw tight, with no expression on his face.

His feet gracefully moved over twigs and leaf's, precious to the silence that could easily be disrupted and reveal where he was.

Another rustle.

Brecee's fingers laced around the trigger and a bead of sweat trailed down his face.

I'll kill a cop. I'm not scared of shit!

"Damn nigga, you on that army shit," Zach's voice broke in. Brecee dropped his gun and turned around.

"What the hell is wrong with you? I could've shot your goofy ass!"

Zach held one of his hands up jokingly, the other was gripping a drink from McDonald's. Brecee eyed Zach with contempt.

"Is that where you were when I almost got caught?"

Zach took one last slurp of his drink then tossed it in the bushes.

"That was after you left. It was on the way. Is it illegal for me to drink something?" Zach opened the car door and slid in.

Just let it go. It was too close of a call.

Breece finally slid in the driver's seat and started up the car. He peered at Zach from the side of his eye.

"Is this a joke to you?" Brecee asked as he turned to glare at Zach. Zach was a rich kid who liked the thrill of the streets. It probably wasn't much of a title since his dad also was a prison leech, but he still left Zach a huge inheritance.

"Nah. But it does seem like things are getting sloppy on your end."

"My end? You were supposed to cover me fool," Brecee said as he hit Zach on the arm.

"What about last time with Monroe? Or Delancey last month?"

There was a brief pause as Zach glared back at Brecee. His eyes were taking in every inch of Brecee, evaluating his every move.

"Are you my mother?" Brecee mumbled.

"I'm sure she'd like you to stay out of trouble," Zach retorted. Brecee started the car, trying to ignore Zach's comment. He knew his mother went to sleep every night with burdens and worries on her mind.

"I'm just taking care of her."

"Isn't that what Jordan is for?"

Brecee gripped the wheel.

"Don't mention his name to me, aight?"

Zach shrugged and looked out into the night.

"At least he takes care of her," he added. The air was stale with unsaid words. Brecee had every intention to bash Zach's head into the window for even alluding to him being sloppy.

Not because he was wrong but because he was right. The truth stung Brecee, but he couldn't let it show. Dealing was all he had and there wasn't a damn thing Zach, his mother, or Jordan could do to stop it.

CHAPTER TWO

Zach and Brecee miraculously made it back to Zach's trashed apartment. They took the backroads and were hidden between the darkness of the trees. The moonlight was still shining by the time Brecee collapsed onto Zach's only couch.

Zach's apartment was a pig's pin. It was the cheapest spot he could find in Brooklyn for a one room. It had a small stairway to the balcony and the walls had gaping holes from unfinished construction. Rats and roaches occasionally made their appearance in the night, and every morning, there was a new leak in the ceiling. Despite the pungent fumes of discarded trash and weed, Brecee saw it as a getaway from his mom's. He loved her but her nagging was becoming more and more excessive.

"Here, man. Might as well get comfortable," Zach said as he handed Brecee a thin blanket. "I don't know why you always crashing here when your moms got that swooped up place in Manhattan."

Brecee rolled his eyes and stared up at the moth-eaten ceiling.

"That's Jordan's money," he muttered. "Besides, you one to talk. Look at how you live. Isn't your daddy a mobster?"

Zach went quiet as he sat on the floor near one of the biggest holes in his walls. His eyes had a faraway look that was misted over with tears, but he blinked them away. That's what Zach and Brecee had in common: missing fathers and confusing pasts.

"That went to my sister. You know that," Zach replied with a clenched jaw. "It was her dream to go to Brown. I don't want her suffering like me."

Brecee had only met Zach's younger sister, Diana, twice. She had a smart mouth with long, brown curly hair. She looked a lot like Zach, except Zach pulled more from his Italian side.

"Glad she got out," Brecee mumbled. "Not all of us can climb out of it."

Zach looked at Brecee with annoyance.

"What are you talking about? There ain't no us in this shit. You know damn well you shouldn't be doing this anymore."

"I've been doing this longer than you," Brecee shot back.

"So. If it weren't for that pity party you swim in, you'd actually stick to what you're really good at."

Zach motioned towards the book peeking out of Brecee's jacket pocket.

"It's just to keep my mind off of things," Brecee added. Zach got up and pulled the book out, studying its tattered cover.

8

"Rules of the law," Zach read with his brows knitted together. He held the book up then tossed it back to Brecee.

"You can fool everyone about you and act like you're this hard-ass thug, but I know you're not," Zach said.

"Just cause it was what I was into a few years back don't mean shit."

Zach sat next to Brecee on the couch with his hands clasped tightly together. He closed his eyes and sat in the growing tension between him and Brecee.

"Is that what Marvin would've wanted?" Zach asked softly. Marvin had been Brecee's older brother. He barely remembered him since he was murdered when Brecee was only eight.

But Brecee remembered seeing him as his last thread of hope right before his dad got arrested. When he was killed, his mom lost every ounce of hope.

"It doesn't matter what he would've wanted. He's dead. Besides, nobody gave a shit about me when I wanted to go to school. Ma poured all that time into Jordan's ass."

Zach got up and headed towards the hall. His shoulders were heavy as he flicked the light off. All Brecee could see was Zach's frail silhouette and the top of his curls.

"We ain't the same man, and you know that," Zach said before quietly walking to his room.

9

Brecee waited until he heard Zach's door close before exhaling. The weight of almost getting killed and then remembering his half-assed ambitions, were too much. He picked his book up and held it in his hands.

He re-read that book a thousand times and knew every single chapter word for word. There had been a time when he swore to Marvin that he'd be something better. He swore he'd do right by his Ma and not fall victim to a bullet.

He broke her heart too many times, though. That burning passion was fizzled out time and time again. Failure and anger became his virtues and before he knew it, he was the man his mother begged him not to be. Slinging drugs and barely escaping the cops.

It wasn't that Brecee had no means to stop; it was that he couldn't see outside of the failure. After his eighteenth birthday, he came to understand that his mom and Jordan saw him as a fuckup. It didn't matter how many times he tried to climb out of that hole; he was branded.

There was beauty in the world of drugs to him, though. He found family. People that admired his skills and looked to him for strategies. As the years ticked by, however, that passion fizzed just like the first.

Zach's word pierced him because he saw him clear as day. He was living a lie and the worst part was that he was too much of a coward to be who he was meant to be.

Brecee closed his eyes and tried to forget his thoughts, again. They were the death to contentment.

Brecee woke up startled from the loud buzzing from his pocket. The morning light was barely peeking through Zach's tattered curtains, but it was already a nuisance to Brecee's eyes. Groaning, he dug the phone out of his pocket half-dreading the unexpected caller.

Jordan.

Brecee lifted himself off the couch and quickly answered the call.

"Bre, where the hell are you?" Jordan barked on the other line. Jordan was Ma's prime son. Her favorite. The only kid of the remaining two that actually went forth with law school and drove around in a shiny car with a decked-out place right in the middle of the city.

Brecee knew how much Ma loved to brag about Jordan's every move.

"Oh, let me show you my Jordan's new car," she'd say to her co-workers at the hospital. The last time Brecee had trailed along with her to work was after he broke curfew and she forced him to pull his weight since the hospital was short staffed.

Even as Brecee was bent over an elderly woman that smelled like piss and cigarettes, he could see the way her hazel eyes

11

crinkled up with joy as she handed her phone, the one Jordan bought, over to her friends.

Brecee could've vomited at the squeals and varicose-veined hands of her co-workers, clasped tightly around the phone. They're smiles stretched across their faces like wounds too deep to sew; they frothed at the thought of a black kid who *finally* did something right.

"Why do you need to know?" Brecee finally answered back as his mind went back to its warfare.

"I had to take a quick flight to Boston for a meeting, remember? You promised you'd keep an eye on her."

Brecee could hear the annoyance in Jordan's uppity tone, as if it was sneakily reminding Brecee that he was just proving to be, yet again, a disappointment. The door down the hallway squeaked open, and Brecee could see Zach's wiry body hobble sleepily towards him.

"Yo, nigga. What's with the theatrics?" Zach asked a little too loud.

"Are you that fool Zach's house?" Jordan screeched.

"Why do you care? Just go to your lil meeting and don't worry about it," Brecee shot back swiftly. Zach walked to the kitchen and drank the remaining drops of orange juice from the carton.

"Listen punk," Jordan spat, his voice lowering to a respectable octave.

"You must be around those white folks, huh?" Brecee taunted him. He could see Zach smirk out the corner of his eye.

"Ma has been up and down with this stomach thing. I'm not expecting you to do anything outside of bumming it with your boys, but for the sake of Ma, at least check to make sure she took her meds."

Brecee held the phone away from his face so Jordan couldn't hear how rapid his breathing was becoming.

I'm not expecting you to do anything outside of bumming it with your boys.

"Who do you think I am?" Brecee asked suddenly. "You and Ma swear you got shit figured out."

Jordan sighed as the ambience in the background got more distorted with loud voices.

"I don't care anymore, Bre. Just do your fucking part."

The phone call quickly ended and Brecee stood up with the weight of Jordan's words making him dizzy.

"You good?" Zach asked from behind him.

"Yeah. Jordan's tripping about Ma, as usual," Brecee started as a lump formed in his throat. "I hate my fucking life."

He didn't expect Zach to react to his pity, especially since it was a common thing for him.

Zach walked over to Brecee with the orange juice carton still in his hand.

"That chrohn's disease still kicking?. I'm sorry to hear that about her," he said, ignoring Brecee's last comment. Brecee looked at Zach and noticed his eyes were full of concern.

"She's fine," Brecee said with no hesitation. He started for the door, but Zach grabbed his elbow.

"You know you my boy, right?"

Brecee grunted and headed out the door.

Right as Brecee started down the street to head to his mom's, the city was waking up. Cars were beeping sporadically and anxious men in suits with multiple coffee cups were rushing into cabs. He was sure that was Jordan. Only Jordan was the type who'd make his own coffee to preserve the environment.

Brecee rolled his eyes at the thought of Jordan. Outside of having two degrees, he still couldn't understand the obsession people had with him.

He looked no different from Brecee; tall, brown skin, buzzed hair, high cheekbones and deep dimples. Some people used to even say that Brecee was a carbon copy of Jordan had it not been for his chin.

"That chin is just like your damn daddy," Ma would say when Jordan and Brecee used to eat dinner together. She'd gloat over Jordan's accomplishments of the day while mentally preparing to cuss Brecee out for getting expelled. Everyone on the block knew Brecee as the troublemaker who could never get it right. Whether it was cheating on tests or bringing a gun to school, he could always tell by the way people's noses and lips would scrunch up exactly what they were about to say.

"You're just like your daddy." The words were as good as poison. They'd hit Brecee like a bullet, rupturing every good intention.

"You think I'm a deadbeat? You think I'm bad? Stupid? A criminal? Fine, I'll show you."

He'd beat brick walls with his bare knuckles until they were bloody with the skin hanging off. The pain was only surface value, though. Nothing compared to how Ma would grin and cup Jordan's face, admiring her own reflection in his eyes.

"My smart baby," she'd coo. Brecee could've flipped the table over. He could've thrown the chairs at the walls and kicked the doors in until everyone finally broke down and listened.

"Aye, yo Bre. What you got on you?" The voice startled Brecee. He looked over his shoulder and realized he'd walked past Hernandez. He was closer to Jordan's age but went downhill after the cops accidently shot and killed his mom. Ever since, he got high on whatever he could get his hands on.

"I'm all out man, sorry," Brecee said before turning around.

"Damn, you sure? I got a bottle I could trade you for."

Brecee looked back over his shoulder at Hernandez, noticing the marks that trailed down his arms. He gripped his crotch over and over as that same desperation that was in every buyer's eyes, burned a hole in Brecee's heart.

"I got you next time," Brecee promised as he turned around and made it down the block. As much as dealing was looked down upon in the neighborhood, he played doctor to a lot of people. People who needed to escape whatever abuse and demons that were haunting them every day. Their eyes would plead and beg for just a momentary release.

It was also the reason Brecee stopped taking the drugs he sold. Nothing that could send a six-foot-five man like Hernandez into a blubbering mess would ever be the antidote for him.

He tried it back when he was nineteen. It started with small doses of coke but pretty quickly escalated to him hunting down dealers and beating them until he got what he needed. Some mornings he'd wake up in parts of New York he didn't even know existed. Those days were dark. Thankfully, Ma and Jordan never found out. If they had, they probably would've thrown him out ages ago.

Brecee finally made it to his Ma's house and stood out in front. It was an older home but in good condition with yellow

16

brick and a brown fence. Jordan always made sure to pay the lawn mowers and keep flowers planted.

Every time Brecee walked through the front door, though, he could always smell that aroma of anger. Ma hated him.

"Ma? I'm home," Brecee called out. He cautiously stepped through the door and peeked around the corner into the front room. Everything was freshly cleaned and vacuumed. A neat handwritten note from the housecleaner was hanging from the wall.

Jordan had landed a job with a new firm and insisted Ma had a housecleaner come in every three days.

"White people shit," Brecee mumbled as he glared at a vase with freshly watered flowers.

"You're one to complain," Ma said from behind Brecee. He jumped as he turned and forced a smile on his face. It was pointless, though; Ma was stone cold.

Despite only being five-feet-two-inches, she could make any man cower in fear. She stepped towards Brecee and sniffed the air.

"You been smoking that skunk?"

Brecee shrugged. There was no use in hiding anything from her at this point.

"I was dropping by to see how you were."

"Dropping by? Negro, you live here. I know it's easy for you to disappear and hang with those friends of yours but thank God, Jordan has my medicine delivered for me. It was up to you I'd drop dead."

"Did you take the medicine?" Brecee asked quietly, his gaze dropping to the floor. Ma rolled her eyes.

"Shut up. Obviously, I did. I made casserole. Come in here and eat."

Brecee followed behind Ma like a lost puppy, swallowing his pride as he sat down at the table. He eyed the several pill bottles spread across the kitchen counter next to a bottle of vodka. Ma set a plate in front of him but caught his gaze at the vodka.

"I was cleaning out the cabinets," she said quickly as she returned to the cabinets with her back turned to Brecee. He kept his eyes glued to the back of her head, waiting for what was coming next. She finally shut the cabinet and grabbed for Vodka, her hand lingering at the cap.

"Your daddy sent a letter in," Ma said softly. She looked over her shoulder at Brecee, already expecting the life to escape his eyes.

"I'm not reading it," Brecee said with a mouthful of casserole.

"Suit yourself. He's been in there seventeen years, guess it don't make no difference. I suppose one of these days you'll at least answer the man back."

18

"Would you? Have you returned any of his calls?" Brecee asked with his forked gripped tightly in his hand. He eyed the vodka bottle again and shook his head.

"Hey, you don't get to question what I do, boy. I raised two boys all on my own thanks to him," Ma yelled. She came close to Brecee with her hands clenched in tiny fists.

"I never said you didn't."

She backed down and sighed, returning to the counter.

"Do what you want," Ma said in a tired voice. She opened a drawer and stuffed the letter in with the mass of others. "Have you heard back from that job at the post office?"

Brecee chewed slowly trying to think of an answer.

"They said they'd call me next Tuesday," he lied.

"That's great! Maybe you'll get it this time. My friend Serena said they're real lenient with who they hire."

"You don't think I could get one anywhere else, do you?" Brecee questioned her with a scowl. She stopped and looked him square in the eyes.

"Do you?"

Brecee stood up abruptly and threw his plate in the sink then headed to the door.

Fuck this place. He already knew the answer to Ma's question. He was just too much of a coward to admit it to himself.

Chapter Three

The wind was picking up as Brecee made his way back into the city. He walked past tons of skyscraper buildings full of ritzy people who wouldn't give him the time of day even if he asked.

"Fucking rich folks," Brecee mumbled as he pushed his way through the crowd. It was an anger that was familiar to him, though. As the years ticked by, Brecee only strayed further away from the likes of Ma and Jordan. Even when he worked as a cashier at the local deli, a job thanks to Jordan, he felt that sting of pessimism as he'd ring up suited up dudes in designer ties.

How are they any better? But it was apparent. He was behind the dirty, finger-printed, glass pane of a broken-down deli that was a run by a fat-bellied Italian.

That was until he met Fredricko.

As usual Brecee filed into work with his heart heavy and slid his hands into the dry, plastic gloves. That day was different, though. The door swung open with ease, not impulsivity, like most businessmen. In walked the smoothest man Brecee had ever laid eyes on.

Caramel, long, curly hair, and a black hat perched to the left. He had a toothpick hanging out of his mouth and a long, gold pendant around his neck. He gazed the room until his eyes fell on Jerry, Brecee's manager. Only, he didn't do anything.

He raised his hand and three more men scattered into the deli with guns tucked behind their backs. Brecee's breath caught in his throat. He was too afraid to call the cops. What if they shot him? Or went after Ma?

Jerry's eyes bulged out of his head at the sight of Fredericko, not the armed men, and he jutted his chin up.

"I got it back here," he stammered. The men looked back at Fredricko like trained puppies, only resuming their quest when Fredricko waved them away. It took a matter of seconds for Fredricko to finally look over in the direction of Brecee.

His eyes took Brecee in slowly, sizing up his oversized, wrinkled work shirt that clearly was handed down from a much larger man. His hair hadn't been cut in months and he still had baby fat on his cheeks.

A soft smile spread across his face, showcasing a variety of gold teeth.

"You the manager?" he teased as he rested his large, calloused hands on the counter. Brecee shook his head quickly and pointed to the back.

"I work for Jerry," Brecee said. A cold sweat poured down his back, but he didn't dare show his fear. "What do you want with him?"

It was bold question but Fredricko seemed to admire Brecee's curiosity.

"We're business partners, you see," Fredricko claimed. "If it weren't for me this raggedy place would be a clump of rocks and dust."

"Maybe it should be," Brecee muttered. "I mean only the fat cats come in here."

Fredricko stared deeply in Brecee's eyes, scanning for a flicker of mistrust; he found none.

"You like working here, kid?"

Brecee briefly looked to the back door where Jerry disappeared with the three-armed men. He spent way too much time at the deli listening to Jerry argue in Italian with his wife and nitpick on how he cleaned the sandwich station. There also was a pungent stench of salami and soured bread.

"I'm not planning on staying here forever," Brecee admitted. Fredricko was charmed. He leaned forward and hit the bottom of the glass divider so that it raised up. Even though he was still a few feet away from Brecee, Brecee knew if he wanted to, he could kill him right then and there.

"I see something in you that reminds me a lot of myself," Fredricko explained softly. "You got that young entrepreneur gleam in your eye."

Entrepreneur?

The word might as well had been candy. It was so far-fetched from the names Ma and Jordan called Brecee.

"You must be thinking of the wrong dude," Brecee said with insecurity leaking into his words. "I ain't got shit to offer."

"Not in no sandwich, obviously. But there's a whole 'nother world out there," Fredricko said. He reached into his shirt pocket and pulled out a black card with a single phone number in glossy, silver writing.

"Call me when this shit gets old."

Right as Brecee took the smooth, black card in his hands, the back door swung open and the three men came out with their jaws tight and small splatters of blood on their shirts. Brecee was in shock as one of them handed a stack of money to Fredricko.

"Where's Jerry?" Brecee blurted out. The three men immediately looked at Brecee with the intent to get him next, but as soon as Fredricko raised that calloused hand, their expressions went blank again.

"What's your name?"

"Brecee."

"How old are you?"

"Twenty-three."

Fredricko nodded and then stuck out his hand. Brecee took it slowly, shaking it with precaution.

"I'm Fredricko Gonzales. This is Louie, Marco, and Donnie. They've been working with me ever since we first landed here."

Brecee looked at the men and noticed the scars and old bullet wounds covering their exposed arms. There was a second of fear until Brecee peered at Fredricko's wide grin and joyful eyes.

"I'll give you a call for sure," Brecee promised. Fredricko and the men quickly filed out of the store, leaving Brecee with a myriad of questions.

He cautiously stepped from behind the sandwich booth and walked to the back door.

"Aye, yo Jerry?"

There was a piercing silence.

Did they kill him? I didn't hear no gun shots.

Brecee eased the door open and found a battered Jerry barely conscious on the floor. His eyes were swollen shut and his arm was dislocated. Anxiety pumped through Brecee's body as he looked down.

Jerry groaned softly but Brecee's pity turned to fascination.

How did a man like Fredricko get so much power?

Brecee's question stayed with him until he finally gave in to the power test of Fredricko Gonzales eight months after he turned twenty-four.

"Yo, Fredricko? I'm outside."

Brecee stood outside the usual hotspot for Fredricko's meetings. It was an abandoned lot where only crackheads and dealers would come. The garage slowly raised up revealing Louie on the other side.

Since Brecee had first met him two years ago, Louie had aged a lot. His shoulders started to cave in, and flecks of grey dominated the dark, kinky fro he had.

"How is it?" Brecee asked as he casually strolled in. Louie looked him up and down. Brecee knew Fredricko's original three grew to despise him ever since Fredricko took Brecee under his wing.

"Damien got caught up."

Damien was a year younger than Brecee but was a lot like Zach. He was careless with money and women.

"Is he dead yet?"

Louie cocked his head to the side of the huge garage where a bloody unconscious Damien was hanging from a rope by his wrists.

"Not sure."

Brecee didn't have time to feel sorry for Damien. Even though he'd been under Fredricko's wing, it had only been three months since Fredricko started considering him for real dealing.

Fredricko was sitting in his usual chair with a pound of coke on his desk. His hair had started to thin, and he had a large beer gut.

"Yo, Fred."

Fredricko grinned and stood up with his arms outstretched.

"My son, come here."

Fredricko embraced Brecee with a long, tight hug that choked Brecee in his loud cologne.

"I heard what happened with Damien," Brecee muttered as Fredricko pulled away.

"That boy. He betrayed me, Brecee."

"You take him out?"

Fredricko lit a cigar up and handed one to Brecee.

"I don't take out the children God sends me. I just discipline."

"That's why you run this city," Brecee said with a smile. Fredricko nodded and blew out a puff of smoke.

"You know you worried me, Brecee."

"What?" Brecee set his cigar down.

"That little weed run? What did I tell you about working with outside people?"

Brecee stared down at his shoes.

27

"I needed quick money. Had to pay an old friend back," Brecee admitted. It was the truth, too. Back when Brecee was strung out he swore he'd pay Dominic, his old dealer back. Dominic was cutting down on the bribes and threatened to hurt Ma.

"Why do you think I'm here? Are you that afraid of me, son?"

"No, no. I just don't want you to think I'm a fuckup."

Fredricko grabbed the pound of coke and dropped it in Brecee's lap. Brecee stared down at the block like it was his past coming back to drown him.

"How long had you been on it?" Fredricko questioned.

Brecee thought to lie but it was no use.

"Barely a year."

"Were you on it when I met you?"

Brecee nodded. "It was the only thing I had going for me."

"That's why you're good with me," Fredricko swore as he tapped the block of coke. "It's safe if you do it when I'm around. But I can't have you messing with these outsiders. They'll have you in prison faster than these crackheads snort this shit."

"Thanks for looking out for me, but I don't snort like that anymore." Brecee tried to place the coke back in Fredricko's hands, but Fredricko pushed his hand back.

"You think I'm dumb? I know you're not weak like them. You got control. You're smart, chino. That's why I want you to take over deals."

Brecee gasped. He could feel Louie stiffen next to him. Louie always dealt the coke.

"What about Louie?"

"Louie and I talked. Don't worry about that."

The coke suddenly felt like a hundred pounds in Brecee's hands. Weed dealing was one thing, but coke on top of him barely being able to fight off his urges was another.

"Brecee," Fredricko called. "You know I wouldn't put you out there to get set up, right? Didn't you tell me how much you hate living at home and how you wanna be drowning in money?"

"Yeah, be up in those nice ass apartments," Brecee muttered as he thought back to the high-rise apartments he'd always pass.

"Then do this, make the money, and start your life, chino," Fredricko urged. He reached out and patted the side of Brecee's face. "I see so much potential and greatness in you. You got this."

Whether Fredricko knew how much Brecee survived off of words or not, it was enough to send happiness through Brecee's body.

"I won't let you down," Brecee promised as he got up and walked away. Louie walked closely behind Brecee with a bag in his hand. As soon as they reached the entrance, Louie handed Brecee the bag with a stern look on his face.

"Be careful with this shit. It's not a game. And definitely not something to share with your goofy friend."

Brecee's heart stopped as he glared back at Louie.

"Yeah, I know about Vallencio's son," Louie added.

"How?"

Louie turned his back to Brecee. "How you think them cops got led away?"

"Thanks—"

"Don' thank me, lil nigga. Be careful. Not only will boss take him out, but you'll be next."

Louie walked back to the garage and closed it swiftly. Brecee looked down at the bag full of coke. He already knew Zach was a dead weight to him. But he was still his friend.

Fredricko was, however, the only person that actually saw good in Brecee.

I'm not fucking this up. I'm not.

Brecee set off back down the street with the bag tightly in his hands as his mind raced about the possibilities that were sure to come.

He would just have to the fight off the urges to use again, even if it killed him.

CHAPTER FOUR

S oft R&B music belted from Naudia's headphones as she finished up her cycling class. She was greeted by the exuberant and sweaty faces of her roommates Myra and Toni. They were chattering about their latest hook-ups as usual and Naudia kept quiet as they waited for the next elevator.

Naudia's phone dinged lightly and she quickly checked it.

Be there in ten. You ready for the movie?

"Who you smiling at, girl?" Toni asked as she tied her braids into a loose bun.

"Probably that lil boyfriend," Myra joked as she playfully nudged Naudia's arm.

Naudia remained quiet since she knew Myra and Toni were the gossiping types. Besides, she knew Brecee wasn't everyone's favorite.

It didn't matter much to her, though.

When they first met, Naudia was at the skating rink with her sorority raising money for the homeless. She was shy by nature but still outspoken. Her Haitian roots came through like fire when anyone tried to undermine her intellect or space.

Things were different with Brecee. He was beautiful to her with a gentle nature.

"What you out here selling?" he asked with a sly smile. He was wearing a faint blue t-shirt that brought out his red undertones beautifully. Naudia was stunned but went right into explaining.

As she spoke, she could feel Brecee taking her in with curious eyes and hanging onto her every word. A strange heat crept up her back enveloping her in infatuation with a complete stranger.

"Why are you looking at me like that?" she asked breathlessly. He reached out and softly touched the top of her hand, brushing his index finger along her knuckles.

"I saw you come in and I just had this feeling come over me," he said with anticipation. "I can't buy nothing from you but I wanna get to know you."

When their eyes met, Naudia felt a deep pull towards him. Her heart and head were in sync as she reached into her pocket and pulled out her phone. His smile was the main thing she could never forget. It stretched across his face with ease and met his eyes with a soft twinkle.

I can't imagine not having him, Naudia thought. Her thought manifested into a full blown relationship a month later. After that, they spent every waking moment together.

None of her family understood it, either. She was the daughter of Manhattan's top financial broker and her mother owned several boutiques.

"What does he do?"

"What school does he attend?"

"Where are his parents from?"

The questions poured out like gushing blood from a wound when Naudia announced she had a boyfriend. She expected there to be light laughter and joyful clapping at the sound of her first relationship, but instead, the piety of her family soured the mood.

Her father's brow deepened into an angry frown line when she answered, "He doesn't have a job at the moment."

His hands tightened around his wine glass as silence hit the air. Naudia's mother knew not to utter a word against her husband in these tense moments, especially since she was usually Naudia's safety net.

But even her voice trembled with fear and rage.

"What are you talking about, Naudia? Did you forget who your father is? How could you disrespect him like that?"

Naudia's father sat with a straight back and clenched jaw as pride shone in his eyes. He enjoyed nothing more than being reminded he was the founder of the Vontane name. It was one of the reasons why Naudia preferred Brecee's calm nature. He held his ground but didn't boast about his achievements.

She wasn't a fool either; she knew there were areas where Brecee lacked. His mother and brother looked down at him like he was the scum of the earth. It shattered her when she finally met his mother. The distraught look in her eyes as she shook Naudia's hand and kept muttering her last name over and over again.

"Vontane? Vontane?"

Naudia knew it was code for, *You're the daughter of Manhattan's biggest name, but you're with him? My son?*

Son might as well be replaced with failure, though. Naudia would dig her nails deep into her skin every time Brecee's mother would downplay his every move.

"I got that job at the deli shop now."

"What more could you expect? It ain't nothing better you can get."

She saw her own mother in Miss Julie Monroe's eyes. A strong woman who brought her kids up, despite the lack of love and support. Naudia was fully aware of her father's countless mistresses and the nights she'd hear her mother softly crying in her room.

On her sixteenth birthday, her father commited the ultimate crime by being seen in public by one of her mother's socialite friends. It didn't matter that Naudia was dressed in her designer birthday dress. Her mother was sobbing in her closet with a pile of purses and unworn shoes that still smelled like the store cluttered around her.

"I can't believe it," she said with smeared mascara on her cheeks. She was such a beautiful woman with high cheekbones and dark brown skin. Naudia hugged her tight and smoothed her hair.

"I know you loved him, Mommy. I know the heartbreak hurts," Naudia gently said as she held her mother. But her shoulders stiffened, and she placed her arms on Naudia's shoulders. Her eyes had a look of confusion and almost laugher.

"The press, baby. The press is going to shit all over my store," she replied. Just as quick as she destroyed her closet, she pushed Naudia off of her and brought herself up from the floor. In a matter of two minutes she redid her makeup and changed into a chiffon, beige dress and slipped into one of the scattered pairs of shoes.

"C'mon, there's guests downstairs. Worst thing you can do is leave a bad taste in their mouths by not showing up."

She reached her hand down to Naudia, not as a token of strength to remind her daughter that life had its downs, but as an urgency to not disrupt their social status.

It was always that day Naudia visioned whenever her mother spoke in favor of her father. Naudia almost had the nerve to laugh in the face of her mother as she dared to question why she'd date Brecee.

"I am a grown woman about to graduate. I think I can handle my own affairs accordingly."

She excused herself that night and left out the backdoor to meet Brecee for their special night walks. It was the night he took her in his arms and kissed her passionately then professed his love.

36

"I may not be ballin' like your folks, but I'ma be somebody. I want you by my side." Naudia initially had an inkling to tell him what happened at dinner. To pour her heart out about how crooked her parents were. But he looked so blissful and free that night as they sat on the balcony of an abandoned bank. All she could do was take his hand and promise to stay when he needed her.

"Hey, baby," Naudia chirped as she ran out to hug Brecee. He was sweaty but managed to have two single flowers in his hand.

"It ain't much but—"

Naudia kissed him and hugged him tightly.

"Come inside, I cooked some spaghetti for dinner."

Naudia knew her parents would choke if they knew Brecee stayed at her dorm from time to time. She managed to keep them out of her school life since she was on a full scholarship and promised to join her dad at his company.

Brecee usually crashed there three days a week but Naudia loved his company.

"Anything new?" she asked as she fixed him a big plate of food. Brecee immediately dug his fork in and savored the first bite. Naudia noticed how he avoided her eyes, a sign that something could be on the horizon.

"Got a new job," he said finally.

"That's so great! I'm so proud of you!"

Naudia hugged and kissed Brecee on the cheek. "Where's it at?"

He chugged a bottle of water halfway through as his eyes once again drifted to the side. He grinned coyly as a coverup to the brief pause.

"A warehouse. Lifting boxes and shit," Brecee said with another big bite. "It pays real good, baby. I'm 'bout to buy you new shoes and clothes."

Naudia laughed as she took a bite of food.

A warehouse job that pays that much?

She didn't want to doubt him right off the bat.

He gets that enough from his Ma and Jordan.

"You don't need to do any of that for me, baby."

"Why? Cause you buy yourself what you want already?"

"You know I like taking care of myself."

Brecee chugged the rest of his water and stared down at his empty plate. His mouth twisted into a grimace but as usual, he pushed it away to not worry Naudia.

"I'm gonna be in the city, too. In those big skyscrapers with a butler and big-ass closet," Brecee said with a childish grin. Naudia could tell by the faraway look in his eyes he was already envisioning himself in the future with brand new shiny furniture and overflowing with money.

She wanted that for him so badly. There was a bitter taste in her mouth, though, that hung like a heavy weight.

"What about your Ma and Jordan?"

There it was. The shot released into the air that obliterated his seasonal happiness. Naudia would hate herself for stomping down on his bright dreamland in his head; but she knew Brecee.

"Screw them," he said forcefully as his upper lip contorted into a scowl. "They don't give a shit about me. Never have."

"Did you tell your Ma about the new job? I'm sure she'd be excited."

"She's never excited about what I do."

It wasn't a lie, either. Anytime Naudia would visit Ma, she'd ask Naudia the same question.

"How did he get you?"

In the occasion that Naudia could hold her tongue, she'd murmur, *"I love him and that's all that matters."*

But the last time Naudia began to restate her answer, Ma reached over and grabbed Naudia's hand like she had just been told a dangerous secret. She leaned in with tears watering her eyes. Naudia could see all the fine lines around her eyes and forehead that were usually concealed by her thick, curly hair.

"He's just like his daddy, sweetheart. He's gonna be just like his daddy."

It wasn't the usual eye-rolling comment followed by a tight-mouthed frown. It was love. It was like Ma was looking into the mirror at a younger version of herself and seeing the forecast of Naudia's future.

Except there was vital truth to Naudia and Brecee that Ma couldn't see: he was so much more than what he did. It was beyond his jobs and lack of money. It was in the way he'd hold Naudia when her father's demands were too much; the way he'd ran across the city just to escort her out of a crazy party.

He loved Naudia to the core and wouldn't dare brush her off the way her father did.

"You've been hurt Miss Julie," Naudia managed to say without tears falling down her face. "But I hope you come to see Brecee the way I see him."

"I just want you to consider all things, baby. I love you," Naudia said as she held onto his wrist. His eyes were faraway again and it left her wondering where he went when his eyes glazed over.

Was it deep thought? Was it pain? Was he reliving the past?

Brecee stood up and kissed Naudia on the forehead.

"I gotta head out, but I love you." He kissed her again on the forehead, this time lingering with his hands gently brushing back her messy hair.

"I love you, too," Naudia said right before he rushed out the door. She sighed as she stared at the mountain of spaghetti, she knew she wasn't going to eat.

Once Brecee was out the dorm, he could feel his lungs on fire. Every breath felt like a knife slicing through him. That's when the itch always appeared.

He swayed back and forth, trying to busy his thoughts to escape the temptation of his worst enemy in the bag.

The air choked him and slapped at his skin as if tempting him to cave in.

"You know I'll take care of you." Brecee could hear Fredricko's words replaying in his mind. His voice echoed in his head like a drum. He raced down the street with the bag hanging limply in his hand as sweat drenched him.

The world was leaning sideways when he finally slid to the ground against an abandoned building and reached into the bag. The coke felt like sand in his hands. He grabbed his credit card and neatly lined it on his hand then snorted it.

A tingling sensation rushed from his head to his toes, making him cry out happily. He let his head fall back against the wall as the night lights appeared to perform for him, glittering in the sky.

He smiled and closed his eyes as every burden finally left temporarily.

"I'ma be rich. I'ma prove 'em wrong," Brecee muttered as he drifted into a stupor of extravagant cars and fancy apartments.

CHAPTER FIVE

*"M*ister Monroe? Breezy Bre? Wake up lil man,"
Steven Monroe said softly as a sleeping Brecee
slowly cracked his eyes open.

"Pops? When you get here?"

Steven held up a satchel with golden light pouring out the top.

"I got everything you need right here, lil man."

The bag lit the entire room in yellow light that was hot to the touch.
Brecee outstretched his short, chubby fingers to touch it. But just as he
finally touched it, Steven grabbed his wrist with a grave look in his
sunken eyes.

The golden halo evaporated from the bag and was replaced by thick,
black liquid that spilled onto Brecee's covers. Brecee screamed and tried
to break away from the ice-cold liquid. Steven grabbed Brecee's wrist
again with superhuman power and lifted him off the bed.

"It's cold on this side son."

Brecee opened his mouth to scream only when he looked to the
mirror all he saw was himself pulling at his own hand.

"Aye, you hear what I said?" Louie's voice barked, dragging Brecee out of his dream. It was always the same dream every time Brecee was about to do illegal things. It was as if his father was communicating with him in his sleep, warning him about what was to come.

The night was nothing but a blur. Louie miraculously found Brecee stopped over a rocky ledge holding onto a deserted coffee mug.

"You better not pull that shit you did last night," Louie warned with a tight mouth. He had to drag Brecee all the way back to his tiny apartment just to clean him up before Fredricko checked in. Brecee was now under the wing of Louie and if anything happened, Louie knew Fredricko would take him out with ease.

"I'm straight."

"Your Ma and brother know what you doing?"

Brecee shook his head as the bright sun burned his irises.

"I'm on my own time."

"No, you on Fredricko's time. If anything goes wrong, he'll hang our asses out back."

Louie's apartment looked like a scene out of a horror movie with a long, black pouch spread from the couch to the dining room table. It had several compartments that were jam packed with different types of drugs from pills to powder. Brecees's eyes took in every pink and purple pill that he was sure would off some customers.

"What the hell is this shit? I thought we did coke."

"You do coke, junky ass. I sell what the market needs."

"I don't do coke," Brecee snapped. He knew last night was a relapse, but he was keen on giving himself passes.

I got a lot of pressure on me. I deserve it here and there.

"Whatever. Dealer never does none of the shit he sells. Why you think there's a market for it?" Louie talked with his eyes glued intently on the pouch. His large, scarred hands traced over each compartment slowly as if he was afraid he missed something. Brecee eyed the rest of Louie's tiny apartment with suspicion.

The couch was a tattered, seaweed green color with the plastic still on; the blinds were ripped sheets and there was a single, flat mattress to the far corner. Brecee knew Fredricko lived in a high-rise at the peak of the city that was always overflowed with beautiful women and never-ending music and drinks.

Louie lived worse off than Brecee.

"Where your share go?"

Louie dropped his hands and finally peered at Brecee. His eyes were bloodshot and the cords in his neck pulsated.

"Why's it any of your business?"

45

Brecee sat back against the couch but didn't take his eyes off Louie. He could feel himself embodying Zach's prying gaze as he took in every detail of the man next to him.

Louie sighed and started to close the pouch.

"Shit ain't for the faint-hearted that's for sure," he mumbled. "Any mistake can cost your life."

"Is that why your boys ain't here no more?"

Louie paused as a tremor passed through his old bones. If Brecee hadn't been mistaken, he could've sworn that Louie resembled a scared little boy who was stuck in a habit he couldn't break.

"He was my boy, Fredricko," Louie said as he set the pouch in a black bag on the table. "He was never vicious. We just wanted out of that low life."

Brecee thought back to his own father and the day he was arrested. There was a look of grief and tranquility as he was thrown in the back of the cop car. The grief swallowed Brecee whole as he screamed and tried to run after him. It was the hint of peace, the acknowledgment that his life was gone, that really haunted Brecee.

"It won't be me," Brecee said aloud right as there was a bang on the door. Louie swiftly got up to open the door. The door swung open to a beaming Fredricko in a flowery shirt with matching jeans. He pulled Louie in for a tight hug, kissing him on the cheek.

"Today's the day, yes?"

Louie nodded stiffly and closed the door with a grunt.

"Yo, Fredricko," Brecee chirped as he stood and held out his hand. Fredricko pulled him in for a tight hug and patted his back roughly.

"Are you sharp, son?"

Brecee nodded. Fredricko motioned for him to sit down on the couch. As soon as they sat down, the couch plastic whistled and sank so low that Brecee wasn't sure if it was an actual cushion.

"I don't want you to worry about today, Brecee," Fredricko said with a hard grip on Brecee's shoulder. "You will be Louie's second in command and all you must do is keep an eye out and make sure nothing funny happens."

Fredricko reached into his pocket and pulled out a small gun. He held it in front of Brecee with a grin that failed to meet his eyes. Brecee saw flashes of his dream of the satchel with golden light that quickly turned to darkness.

The gun felt like a token of death as Brecee slowly took it in his hands. He'd never really held a gun like that before. As he looked back to Fredricko, he saw all the warmth disappear from his eyes. He was replaced with a robot who exuded hate.

"This here is my lifeline," Fredricko said in a low tone. "If anything happens, no one is to be led back to me."

Fredricko tapped the gun with a forceful finger. His eyebrows rose into a jester-like grin that hinted at all his crimes.

"This isn't just for you. This is for me, too. Isn't that right, Louie?"

Brecee looked back at Louie who stood like a fallen solider. He nodded stiffly.

"Boss don't go back on his word."

"He had the humblest of friends, too. They paid the price for my freedom because they knew they were forever in debt to me," Fredricko said with a small shrug.

"I saved them from the slums. They could've been living at the bottom of the barrel for the rest of their lives, but I reached in and plucked them out."

Fredricko reached into his shirt pocket and pulled out a tiny plastic bag with coke in it. He waved at Louie and without hesitation Louie offered a clear tray.

Fredricko spread the coke out and separated it with a card. He then shuffled a small dose to Brecee and handed him a rolled up one-hundred-dollar bill. Brecee could see Louie stare down at him with contempt, but he didn't have much of a choice.

Brecee sniffed the coke up quickly then rubbed his nose. Fredricko took the next line and grunted loudly and licked the remaining residue from his finger.

"I see myself in you, Brecee," he continued. "You're like a lost lamb and I am the Shepard. I was the lamb once, too. My family hated me. They told me I was gonna die in the streets. But look at me. Fucking look at me."

Fredricko grinned with his arm outstretched. Brecee noticed the splotches of blood on his shirt.

"You seem free."

"I make freedom, son."

Brecee nodded and stared down at his wrists like he was expecting to see chains.

Am I free?

Trepidation flew through Brecee's body. For once he felt smaller than before. He felt like a child. He felt the same emptiness that engulfed him when Ma told him his Pops was in prison for murder.

Naudia's face passed through his mind, too. Her soft smile and the way she'd wrap her small arms around him.

I gotta do it for her.

Brecee stood up and shoved his hands in his pockets.

"I'm ready when you are."

He was ready to show his boss who he truly was.

The job was like nothing Brecee expected. He kept waiting on Louie to stop the car in a dark, seedy ally with customers waiting behind the dumpsters like usual. But instead, they stopped at huge mansions full of rich, white people in expensive clothes. Most times they'd be too drunk to even notice Louie and Brecee waltz in. The music would be blasting, and women were dancing and grinding on each other, some naked and others barely conscious.

"Just keep moving," Louie said over the music. "If you stop, they'll find a way to take money off you."

Louie explained it was how the kid before got his teeth knocked out. He saw a topless girl and ran over to her and before he knew it, she stole six grand worth of drugs out of his pockets.

Fredricko beat him until he was unrecognizable.

The rest of the walk was always to a quiet room as the customer would lazily pull out a wad of cash. Sometimes they'd try to short-end Louie. But Louie would pull out a gun and point it at their balls.

"Either you give me the fuckin' money, or you won't be fuckin' any of these bitches."

Brecee's blood went cold at the sound of Louie's words. He was ruthless but never spoke like that around Brecee. The money was always slid into the bag with shaky hands and Louie would throw their delivery into their laps. As they walked out,

Louie's shoulders would stay loose and his stride confident. People would make way for him as if he was a god.

"Damn, you a cold-ass nigga," Brecee said once they were back in the car. Louie cracked a smile, the first expression other than anger that Brecee saw on his face.

"You'll catch on."

"You weren't always like that?"

"Not when I was a goofy-ass twenty-five-year-old."

"Oh, you calling me goofy?"

"You goofy for wanting to be a part of this," Louie said with a look of disappointment. "You know he had me follow you before he reached out."

"Where at?"

Louie started the car up again and drove with his long fingers laced around the wheel.

"That community college. What were you trying to get into?"

Brecee sighed and stared out the window as the high from their dealing faded away.

"Surprisingly, criminal law. I wanted to be those good lawyers that helped folks like my dad get out."

"Your dad innocent?"

Brecee went quiet briefly as he recalled all the times Ma cursed his dad's name. He hated his dad but when he was a kid, he wanted nothing more than to be just like him.

"He did a lot of bad shit. But even though I hate him, I always felt it was a set up. Thought that if I did what I needed to, I could help him."

"So why aren't you?"

"I'm a piece of shit, nigga! Don't no college want a drop-out with my record."

"I told myself the same thing," Louie said as he parked the car in front of their next stop. "I swore up and down I couldn't do it. That was a dumb. But all these years I was the brains behind all of Fredricko's shit, I realized I probably could've had a chance."

Louie cut the car off and turned to look at Brecee. His eyes were heavy but set intensely at Brecee.

"I got a son that don't even know I exist because of this shit."

"I'm already here, man. What you want me to do?"

Louie nodded and opened the door. As soon as they both were out the car, Brecee saw Louie was back to his hard exterior.

"Let's go. Your turn now."

Chapter Six

Naudia noticed a light in Brecee's eyes when she saw him again. His shoulders didn't slump over when he sat down. He was lighter.

"Did I miss something?" she asked as they sat on the balcony of an elegant restaurant. Naudia was used to places with high class menus and drinks she could barely pronounce; Brecee, however, wasn't.

"Can't I just take my girl out on a nice date for once?" Brecee said with a grin as he gazed at the menu. The waiter came back with a fresh bottle of wine that was placed in ice.

"Have we decided on what we'll have?"

Brecee slammed the menu shut and slid it across the table to the wiater.

"Yeah, we'll take the special."

Naudia kicked Brecee under the table.

"Uh, Brecee?"

"It's fine, baby, I got it." Brecee winked and smiled politely at the waiter. As soon as the waiter whisked around the corner, Naudia leaned in with a frantic look in her eyes.

"Babe, if you're feeling some kind of pressure to impress, please don't. This is absolutely ridiculous. You just started working at the warehouse."

Brecee cupped Naudia's chin in his hand, gently rubbing his thumb against her cheek. Her face relaxed finally.

"You gotta trust me, baby. I told you I was gonna start taking care of you."

"But the warehouse can't possibly pay that much, right?"

Brecee took the wine bottle out of the ice and poured a glass for him and Naudia.

"I get bonuses for extra work."

Naudia sipped slowly, not fully believing Brecee.

"Bonuses? What kind of work do you do there anyways?"

"It's a warehouse, babe!"

"Yeah but there's different types pf warehouses. My dad owned this one that shipped office supplies—"

"So, we back on them again."

Naudia paused and realized Brecee's easy smile was gone. She reached across the table but he pulled his hand away.

"I didn't mean it like that, Brecee."

"You don't think I got pressure to live up to your daddy's money?"

"I never asked you to, Brecee."

Sweat started to trickle down the sides of Brecee's face and his leg shook. He grabbed ice from the bucket and started to eat it. Naudia sat back in her seat as she watched him go from normal to sporadic in a matter of seconds.

She knew it wasn't completely out of the blue, either. Her father had met Brecee when they were on their way to lunch. Naudia saw Brecee walking and waved him over. As much as she loved Breceee, there was a part of her that regretted waving him over. He was wearing baggy jeans and white t-shirt that clearly never felt the heat of an iron.

Naudia could feel her dad's disgust without even looking at him.

"Dad, this is Brecee, my boyfriend," Naudia said with her eyes glued on Brecee. Brecee offered his hand but her dad hesitated.

"This is the warehouse boy?"

Brecee dropped his hand abruptly.

"Daddy, please." Naudia whipped around in hopes of exerting mercy from her dad but he ignored her.

"Get back in the car, Naudia. You can see your little friend later."

Naudia looked back at Brecee helplessly.

"It's fine. I gotta get to work anyways." Brecee quickly made it across the street and disappeared into a sea of people.

Once Naudia slid back in the car she glared over at her dad. He was scrolling on his phone with his lips pursed.

"How could you? You're so rude to him and—"

"Are you sure the boy works at a warehouse? Looks to me like he slings drugs."

"Brecee Monroe. His name is Brecee Monroe."

Her dad finally looked over at her from the tops of his glasses.

"Driver, let's go."

Naudia knew not to take anything her parents' criticism about her life seriously. Both of them were lost in trying to maintain their social statuses after her father's numerous affairs. But it was in the way that her father sized Brecee up.

If there was anything her dad was good at detecting, it was someone's true nature.

Slinging drugs? My Brecee would never!

However, the thought worsened as she sat across from Brecee in one of the most expensive restaurants in the city and watched him sweat and shiver.

Brecee rubbed the ice over his face, completely ignoring Naudia's teary eyes.

"Brecee? What's going on?"

"It's so hot," Brecee muttered.

The waiter came back with their trays of food, but Naudia didn't have much of an appetite. For once, she feared her dad might be right about something.

Brecee stared at the food and got up abruptly. "I gotta pee."

Brecee stumbled into the main restaurant and he knew the dinner guests were eyeing him suspiciously.

Fuck them. I got three stacks on me.

As soon as brecee reached the bathroom, he slammed the door shut and pulled out a pouch of coke.

"Just need...one...line."

He pulled out his credit card and separated one line, then sniffed it quickly. He stumbled back and hit the wall as his body finally calmed down. The rage and anxiety settled, and the euphoria took the forefront.

He staggered to the mirror and patted water on his face.

I gotta keep it together. I can't let Naudia down like that no more.

Once Brecee settled back to the table, the night flew by. Naudia got quieter as the date went on, and when Brecee walked her back to her dorm, she stopped and stared him deep in the eyes.

Brecee was always reminded how beautiful she was when she looked at him like that. Her curly hair was big and framed her face and the green silk dress she was wearing hugged her petite figure perfectly.

"How are you so beautiful?" Brecee asked as he moved in for a kiss. Naudia stopped him.

"Brecee. You wouldn't lie to me about what you do, right?"

Brecee's heart raced but he knew he had to keep it cool.

"Of course not."

"What was that today? Why were you acting like a crackhead, then suddenly got better when you got back from the bathroom?"

Shit, does she know? There ain't no way. If I tell her it would only confirm what her folks say about me.

"I get anxious sometimes. I used to take meds after my dad got locked up, but they messed with my sleep," Brecee lied. It wasn't a complete lie, though. He did have to use medicine to calm his nerves after his dad went to jail. He'd have awful nightmares and keep his Ma up all night.

Naudia's worries slowly left.

"Okay. I love you."

"I love you more."

Brecee kissed Naudia passionately then watched her walk into her dorm. He had a weird, heavy sensation in his chest.

Naudia loved him like no person ever had, yet he was lying to her. She trusted him and he was making her out to be the fool.

He couldn't let her find out. It would break her.

CHAPTER SEVEN

Jordan sat anxiously by the front door with his phone tightly in his hands. The night before he had gotten an unexpected call from Brecee, explaining he wanted to have dinner "as a family."

It was strange for Brecee to behave that way. Jordan had the special talent of sniffing out bullshit when it appeared at his doorstep. And as he said impatiently with a million thoughts racing through his head, the doorbell finally rang.

Jordan hastily opened it with his frown already placed on his face. He was exceptionally surprised, though.

"Hi, bro," Brecee chirped in a brand new button-down and cream pants. He pulled Jordan in for a tight hug, rubbing off a loud cologne. Jordan pulled away in disbelief.

"Nigga, what the hell?"

Brecee stepped inside with a huge gift bag in his left hand.

"Where's Ma? I got her a little something."

Jordan closed the door with caution.

"Now, wait a minute—"

Ma came waltzing in the front room with shock on her face. Jordan expected her to cross her arms and roll her eyes as usual, but she held her arms open and hugged Brecee tightly.

"What in the world?" she exclaimed with a huge smile.

"I look good, don't I?"

Jordan rolled his eyes as Brecee handed Ma the baby pink gift bag. Ma laughed giddily and reached inside.

"Brecee, oh my God!" Ma pulled out a cream Prada bag. Jordan's mouth gaped open in disbelief, followed by contempt.

"Do you like it? I know you always be looking at those magazines with bags and shit," Brecee said with a huge grin. Ma was perplexed but too happy to even question it.

"I love it, Brecee. I got dinner on the stove. Let's eat."

Jordan, Ma, and Brecee all sat at the table together for what seemed like years. Ma's attention and admiration had been transferred to Brecee as he recalled the success and adventures of his new warehouse job. Jordan ate his spaghetti quietly as his thoughts raced.

A prada bag on a warehouse check?

Jordan cleared his throat. "I'm glad the job is working out," Jordan said. "And paying well, apparently. Aren't those Prada bags like two thousand dollars?"

"Got that one on sale," Brecee added quickly.

"Yeah, but why the rush? I usually buy Ma all types of beautiful earrings and clothes when I travel abroad."

Ma touched Jordan's hand gently. "Jordan, baby, I know you're just being the big brother. But I think it's a good sign that Brecee is thinking of his Momma. Afterall, I raised y'all with no help. It's the least a son could do."

Brecee nodded in agreement as he took a gulp of his water.

"I couldn't agree more, Ma," Brecee said. "Also, Jordan, I think I learned a thing or two about saving from you."

Jordan smirked with his left brow raised.

"Is that so?" he asked with a condensing tone. "Because if you did, then you'd know it's wise to wait three checks in before lavish spending. Nice pants, too. Calvin Klein?"

Brecee laughed.

"Yeah, they sure are. If you like em, maybe I'll get you a pair."

Jordan and Brecee glared at one another across the table. The home phone rang, suddenly making Ma jump.

"Y'all better stop that. I gotta get the phone, it might be Anna."

As soon as Ma was out of sight, Jordan reached across the table and grabbed Brecee by the collar. His nostrils were flared and his eyes had more rage in them than Brecee had ever seen. Jordan was prone to rough-handling Brecee after his many fuckups, but Ma never let him throw a punch.

"Get your fuckin' hands off me," Brecee said through gritted teeth.

"I know Ma been sick of your shit and is just hoping for the best, but I'm not. I see you exactly for what you are, and I know exactly what you're capable of." Jordan pushed Brecee back into his chair.

"What's that supposed to mean?"

"A prada bag, nigga? Do you think I'm stupid?"

"Nah. I guess you would know since its all you buy them white girls you stay running after."

Jordan grabbed a glass and threw it at Brecee but he ducked just in time.

"Let me find out you're lying about this warehouse job. I swear to God Brecee, if you let Ma down one more time—"

"Why can't you just be happy for me? Or least hope I'm doing better?" Brecee's voice shook as his fingers gripped onto the edges of the table.

"Be happy for you? I let that shit go a long time ago after you broke Ma's heart again and again. I've been taking care of her all these years and I won't let you bring her down another time."

Jordan's patience had waned over the years. He worked longer hours and called off relationships and trips just to ensure Ma was taken care of. Her love and happiness were the most important thing to him. He couldn't trust Brecee for one moment.

"I love, Ma, too."

"No, you just want us to tell you how great you are when you ain't shit."

Brecee stood up with his fists clenched. He could hear Ma chattering happily on the phone.

"Tell Ma I had to go."

Brecee turned to walk out but Jordan grabbed his arm. Brecee looked over his shoulder at Jordan and saw that he was shaking with tears in his eyes.

"Brecee, please don't end up like him. Not for Ma's sake. For your own."

For the first time, Brecee saw a trace of love in his brother's eyes. He yanked his arm back.

"I got myself. Just take care of Ma."

Brecee headed straight for the door and walked out into the street with his thoughts weighing on him. He knew he messed up but there was no going back this time.

The streetlights were starting to fade to a burnt yellow and Brecee reminisced about the times when he and Jordan would ride their bikes up the street just before it started getting dark. They were young and had not one worry. They'd laugh and chase after each other. Some nights Brecee would crawl into Jordan's bed because his nightmares were too much. He loved Jordan, and back then, he was sure Jordan loved him, too.

CHAPTER EIGHT

It had been a few weeks of pure bliss for Brecee when the high of being on top of the world started to fizzle. He noticed it in the way Naudia and Ma would praise him for his come up but also had a worried, questionable glint in their eyes. It infuriated him. And the only thing that could keep his impulsive nature calm was the very thing he sold: coke.

Brecee promised himself he'd keep it at a safe minimal, but every deal left him shaking and scared. The coke would rush through his body and ease his nerves while still making him feel invincible.

"It's like I'm on top of the fucking world," Brecee told Fredricko as they sat out on Fredricko's balcony. It was a sweltering hot day with barely a breeze and Fredricko's maid served them fresh margaritas.

"That's what it means to live as a king," Fredricko said with a smirk. "All of the ones beneath us look up and wish they could be us."

"People always looked down on me. Ma and Jordan. 'Bout time they respected me," Brecee said as he sipped his margarita. The last conversation he had with Jordan kept replaying in his head. That petrified look Jordan had. It didn't get any better after that, either.

"Is that brother of yours still snooping?" Fredricko asked. He was wearing a button-up shirt that was only buttoned at the top with his large belly hanging out. Brecee noticed the dark circles and thin, veiny skin in the daylight. Fredricko's lips were cracked and his arms had faint scars from years of drug abuse.

"He's just concerned," Brecee said. He knew Jordan had connections to find out the truth. He blackmailed a manager at Reggies Warehouse to cover for him in case Jordan landed on the idea that Brecee was actually lying.

"Blood means nothing you know," Fredricko said flatly. "A brother would never question you if he believes in you."

"I've fucked up so much, though."

Fredricko ripped his shades off and leaned over to Brecee. The cords in his neck were sticking out and his thin lips curled into an O shape.

"Then what kind of asshole is he, huh? I see you, Brecee. You're the smartest one I know. You're a fucking legend." Fredricko grabbed his bowl of coke and neatly lined up a row then snorted it. He knocked his fist onto the small coffee table between him and Brecee, and the maid came running over with a towel. She dabbed his mouth, but he grabbed her by the waist and pulled her onto his lap. She laughed but Brecee could see the fear in her eyes.

"You can have whatever you want in this world," Fredricko breathed. "Lucy, get me the key."

The maid, Lucy, quickly ran into the apartment and returned shortly with a single, white key. Fredricko snatched it from her then got on his knees with the key extended. Tears welled in his eyes.

"Never have I ever met someone so loyal yet so young. I want to give you the gift of freedom. So, you can live without the hatred of others."

"What are you—"

Fredricko pointed to the balcony right next to his own with a wide smile. Brecee's heart sank into his stomach.

"I got a place?"

"In the city," Fredricko replied. Brecee grabbed Fredricko and hugged him as hot tears trailed down his face. The day no longer felt real. Instead, he really was king and had earned his rightful throne.

Who's the fuck up now?

The apartment was like something out of a movie: elegant white walls, white carpet, huge bedrooms, and an accent wall of an Italian renaissance paintings.

"I can't believe this," Naudia said as she stood in the middle of the living room. Fredricko already had the place fully furnished, so Brecee wouldn't have to worry about it.

"Right? Just like my dreams."

Naudia felt uneasy, though. Everything in the apartment, although beautiful, felt fake with an ulterior motive. She was so glad that Brecee was happy but still extremely worried that something else was lurking.

"So, you moved out just like that?"

Brecee shook his head and sat on the huge, red couch on the wall. He patted the cushion next to him and Naudia sat stiffly beside him.

"Not exactly. I'll send for my things, though."

"You'll send for your things'?" Naudia repeated. "Who are you right now, Brecee?"

"Happy as hell. Why aren't you? I got a good job, I'm out my Ma's house, and I got you that brand new bracelet." Brecee pointed at the sparking diamond bracelet on Naudia's thin wrist.

"Yes, I'm thankful. But I'm also not dumb. This is a seven-hundred-dollar bracelet and God knows how much this place cost—"

"It's my place. It's none of your damn concern, Naudia."

"You work at a warehouse, Brecee, and within a few weeks, you come up like this?" Naudia looked around the living room in disbelief. "Something ain't right."

Brecee stood up angrily and walked to the mini bar by the kitchen. His hands were starting to shake as his body ached for coke.

"You acting just like them," he whispered. "You acting exactly how you promised you wouldn't."

"Brecee, I love you. That's why I'm asking these things. I'm worried."

"You don't think I can be good enough like your rich-ass family?"

"Stop it, Brecee!"

Brecee turned around and threw a glass of vodka against the wall. Naudia screamed and staggered back, falling into a fluffy chair.

"You think I'm a fuck-up who can't ever do anything right, huh?"

Naudia started to sob into her hands.

"Shit, baby." Brecee ran over to Naudia but she pushed him away. She grabbed her purse off the floor and ran to the door. Brecee raced after her with sweat drenching his body.

"Naudia!"

"Let me tell you something," Naudia said swiftly with her finger pointed at Brecee. "I loved every part of you. I didn't care what people said. I sacrificed so much to be with you because I saw all the incredible qualities you had. But I'm not gonna act like I don't see something fishy going on."

Brecee steadied himself by holding onto Naudia's arms. The heat was causing him to feel loopy.

"Just... trust me."

Naudia took Brecee's chin in her hand and kissed his forehead.

"Please come back to me safe."

Naudia pulled herself away and took off down the long, winding staircase.

Jordan sat at his desk flipping through case files when there was a knock on his door.

"Come in."

"Uh, Mister Monroe, there's a Naudia Vontane here to see you," Jordan's assistant said through the crack of the door. Jordan set his files down and waved her in.

Naudia brushed past the assistant.

"Hi, Jordan."

"Naudia, hey. Are you okay?"

Naudia set her purse down on Jordan's desk then sat on the couch next to his desk.

"Have you heard from Brecee?" she asked. Jordan sighed and sat back in his chair.

"I saw him last week. He came for dinner and bought Ma a Prada bag."

Naudia gasped. "A real Prada bag?" Jordan nodded and noticed the dazzling bracelet on Naudia's wrist. They locked eyes as the inevitable passed between them.

"Naudia, you're a really amazing girl," Jordan began. "But I always felt you were too good for him."

"Don't you say that to me. I'm not here to hear you bash Brecee. I love him with all my heart," Naudia shot back.

"Okay, then why are you crying? Why do you think like you don't trust the words you're saying?"

Naudia inhaled and stared across Jordan's office.

"Brecee... got a new place," Naudia said softly. "It's a high-rise."

Jordan slammed his fist on the table.

"I fucking knew it. He's not working at no damn warehouse."

"But what if he is? Maybe—"

"Naudia, come on. You're too smart to even consider that. Especially knowing who your dad is."

Naudia's blood was boiling. "He had no influence over me. Instead of accusing Brecee, why not just figure out what's really going on."

Jordan fell silent and ran his fingers across his desk. He turned his chair away from Naudia.

"It's not that I don't love him. He's just never gotten things right," Jordan said. "I don't want you to get hurt, either."

Jordan turned back around.

"Naudia, I'm not gonna stop you from being with him, however, I want you to be prepared for the letdown. Because with Brecee, it's inevitable."

Naudia tore her gaze away from Jordan. She knew in her heart something was off but didn't want to admit it.

"What's gonna happen to him then?" Naudia aksed with tears falling down her cheeks. Jordan grabbed two Kleenex and slid over in his chair to Naudia. She started to cry softly and dabbed her eyes with the Kleenex. Jordan breathed in sharply, trying to fight back his own tears.

"I'm praying to God that it's nothing that'll leave him in prison," Jordan said as he gently took Naudia's hands. "For your sake, until I get to the bottom of it, please keep your distance."

"But I'm all he's got!" Naudia cried.

"Look, we're in the hot spot for drug dealing—"

"Brecee ain't no drug dealer."

"How'd he afford all these things in such a short span of time?"

Naudia shook her head and stared down at her white sneakers.

"How did he get into all this?"

"I wish I had an answer, Naudia. I really do."

Naudia left Jordan's office with a knot in her stomach. She hated not knowing what to do. If Brecee were to be arrested, or worse, killed, Naudia couldn't imagine how she'd carry on. He was her everything. Even though he made a lot of mistakes, he loved her deeper than any guy ever had. She didn't want to just abandon the life they were slowly building.

She especially didn't want to end up in a loveless marriage like her parents. Naudia wanted a life of happiness and overflowing love, regardless if Brecee had a lot of money or not. She wanted Brecee. Only Brecee.

"Please, God, keep my Brecee safe," Naudia whispered as she made the long walk back to her dorm. The days were uncertain and Naudia was scared the love of her life was entering into a dark world where no one could save him. The only thread of hope she had was that Brecee wouldn't put himself in a position to lose her.

Brecee was racing down a dark street as flashing lights and loud voices carried. His lungs were about to give out for running so far.

"I can't run no more," he breathed as his feet began to sink in thick, black tar. Fear was in Brecee's eyes as his entire body became stuck in the tar.

"Stop right there!" The loud voice demanded. "Hands over your head!"

"I can't move! I can't move!" Brecee cried. The dark, shadowed figure fired a shot into the air and it hit Brecee in the shoulder blade. He started to cry but no noise came out.

"Let him sink. He'll never get out of that anyways," the voice said. Soon, Brecee was in pure darkness with only the sound of his heartbeat in his ears.

Every time he tried to speak his throat closed up and his body sunk deeper and deeper. He tried to move his feet to feel for the bottom but there was nothing. Eventually his body tired and became fully emerged in the thick, black tar.

All noise ceased and he became what he knew he was: nothing. He had no thoughts, heartbeat, or vision. He was a speck amongst the other particles inside the tar.

"Wake up, Brecee. Wake the fuck up." It was the final thought before he shifted to unconsciousness.

Brecee woke up with a loud gasp. His chest was tight, and he was covered in sweat. It was just after five a.m. and the birds were beginning to chirp.

"Just a dream," he muttered to himself. Except his body had chills.

Was he nothing?

CHAPTER NINE

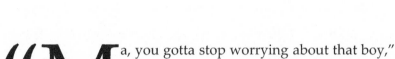

"Ma, you gotta stop worrying about that boy," Jordan whined as he sat across from Ma. He had his workbooks stacked around him while Julie sat near the window on the new couch Jordan bought her.

Her eyes had that faraway look that Jordan recognized as her wondering where Brecee was. Even though chaos seemed to follow him, and he added nothing but stress to Julie's life, he was still her son.

"You wouldn't understand," Julie replied as she took a sip of her fresh lemon tea. "You're not a mother."

"He's my brother, though. Obviously, I love him."

Jordan scribbled notes on some of the papers but knew it was no use. When Ma was worried it dampened the whole day. He loved everything about his Ma because she represented everything he was; sharp, smart, and solitary.

Jordan had his pick of women ever since he got into law school. His classmates would throw themselves at his feet, but he didn't care . He already knew he needed a Michelle Obama over just a pretty face to look good on his arm. He wanted someone exactly like Julie Monroe.

Julie sighed and set her tea down as the line in her forehead softly loosened.

"That boy just causes me grief. Doesn't he know it flares up my condition?" Julie was lying, though. She refused to tell the boys, but she'd been sick long before Stephen was arrested. She always speculated that it was the affairs and never knowing where he was that made her fall ill. Either way, Brecee embodied every part of Stephen and it made her sick.

Julie glanced over at Jordan as he sat with his legs tightly crossed and a pen over his ear.

He's just like me, Julie thought with pride. It was a pain to even acknowledge, but Julie always knew she preferred Jordan to Brecee. It was something about when they were both young and Jordan would do exactly what he was told. Brecee was a wonderer on the other hand. He'd hear what she said but chose to linger in the forbidden places like the dryer or backyard.

"Brecee, why don't you listen?" Julie would yell when he'd come back from school covered in paint and dirt. Jordan would always be standing next to him, still intact with a smug look on his chubby face.

It was wrong to make favorites but how could she not? Brecee was defiant. He loved his father so hard. Harder than

78

Jordan. He'd cry himself to sleep and still whisper about his dad in his dreams. Julie knew that type of heartbreak was unamendable.

"Ma, what is it?" Jordan asked.

Julie wasn't sure what to say. Should she tell him the truth of how she loved him more? Or does he already know?

"I love, Brecee. I really do," Julie said with a wince. "I just don't understand him."

Jordan was quiet as he pulled his pen from over his ear.

"Did you hear something from his mentor?"

"No. He's been doing good."

"Are you sure about that?"

"Why? You know something I don't?"

Jordan shrugged his shoulders and got up to sit next to Julie. He cracked his knuckles and pursed his lips, a sign his mind was in deep thought.

"Ma, he hasn't been home in weeks. You remember what happened last time he was gone, right?"

"Don't get me worrying any more than I already am, Jordan. Besides, I think he listened last time when I got on him."

"Whatever you say."

Julie grabbed Jordan's arm frantically before he could budge. His jaw was clenched in annoyance.

"Baby, what is it?" Julie gently touched Jordan's cheek and his face softened.

"I don't trust him, Ma. I don't want you to get your hopes up again."

Julie let her hand fall back into her lap and curled up into a ball to resume looking out the window. No matter what hope she had for Brecee, he always found a way to break her heart.

Just like his daddy.

CHAPTER TEN

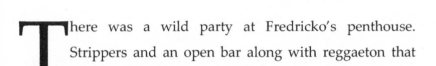

There was a wild party at Fredricko's penthouse. Strippers and an open bar along with reggaeton that painted the night.

Fredricko sat on a huge, purple couch with lion tracings as two strippers were under each of his arms. He was out of his mind drunk but full of happiness. Brecee landed him the best deal of his career: two million in one night. Fredricko was well known in the area, but he wasn't a family name type of man. He only had his loyal pawns who could execute his plans.

Brecee was in charge of the next few deals and managed to shed his 'little boy' status.

"Brecee, my boy," Fredricko said with his glass of vodka raised. "You've made me the proudest dad ever."

Brecee raised his own glass and winked at Fredricko. He finally got everything he wanted in the span of four weeks. Fredricko gave Brecee the keys to a luxury apartment right next to his own and let him drive the cherry red Ferrari he kept in his garage.

"Give it a year and it's yours. I just need to know you can hold this out," Fredricko said the night before. Brecee knew it was well deserved, too; he saved Fredricko's ass after all.

It was a usual deal. Brecee and Louie showed up to a huge mansion, only this time there was no party. The buyer was an older Scottish man by the name of Carson O'Reilly. He was just over seven-two and had a few scuffs of hair left on his head.

"I'm here for Fredricko," Brecee announced to the bodyguard at the door. Louie and Brecee filed in as practiced. Louie taught Brecee how to walk like he was ready to shoot anyone who crossed him.

"It's harder when you a pretty boy, but you'll manage," Louie had told Brecee.

Brecee found a way to settle his face in a grimace that was both neutral and intimidating. They glided in after the bodyguard and found O'Reilly sitting in a lavish office with brown walls.

There were black and white paintings of stone-faced men and a few stuffed ducks and turkeys on the walls.

"It's the family heirloom," Carson said with a chuckle as he hobbled over to Brecee. He was thin and his hands were thin with bulging veins.

"Must be nice. Only thing my dad left me was debt," Brecee said. Carson laughed heartily and gently took ahold of Brecee's arm.

"You must be his new addition," Carson assumed as he glanced over at Louie in the corner. "Got sick of his old crew, eh?"

"New people, old rules," Brecee said softly as he dropped a heavy bag on the floor.

Carson nodded with his eyes avoiding Louie and Brecee. He walked back to his desk and pulled out three stacks of money and handed them to Louie.

"Tell him I send my love."

"Wait."

Brecee stared down at the stacks as Fredricko's voice blared in his head.

"Don't you ever settle for three stacks when you're selling my best shit."

Brecee held the stacks up in the air. "I know this isn't all you're giving my man."

Louie nudged Brecee from behind.

"What the fuck you doin'? Carson's an OG."

Brecee stood his ground, though. He couldn't go back on his demand now.

Carson looked between Louie and Brecee before bursting into laughter.

"You young boys really are bold," he said as he shuffled closer to Brecee. "You accusing me of short-handing?"

"You're an heirloom kinda man who stays locked away in the middle of nowhere. So yeah, I am accusing you."

Carson's goofy smile quickly faded to a scowl and he clapped his hands. The doors burst open as four men with guns came rushing.

"Yo, Carson. He's new. Don't do us like this," Louie tried to plead. Carson kept his beady eyes on Brecee though.

"This one isn't new. He hasn't moved one muscle out of fear," Carson said with his eyes squinted.

Brecee reached into his pocket and grabbed his gun.

"I may be new, but I know all about you and Fredricko. You never paid your last half."

Brecee was in deep water now. It was true, though. He overheard Fredricko foaming at the mouth over Carson never paying him his rightful dues.

If I can get that tonight I'll be set.

Brecee pulled his gun out and pointed it at Carson.

"Brecee!" Louie yelled.

"Boss!" The armed men barked as they unlocked their guns. Carson held his hand up, though, as a smile finally broke out on his wrinkled face.

"I did have a small portion to pay him back. Consider it done."

The armed men lowered their guns in amazement as Carson went back to his desk and pulled out several more stacks. He motioned for Louie to grab the money. Brecee also walked over to slide the coke on the desk along with an extra pouch of ecstasy.

"Tell Fredricko I said thank you for the warning."

Louie paused, taking in Carson's smiling face. Brecee's high was interrupted as that clouded look on Louie's face made him question if the extra money was a good thing.

"Let's go," Louie ordered as they left.

As soon as they finally got back in the car, Louie punched Brecee in the nose. It came out of nowhere and felt like a truck ran over Brecee's head. Louie's nostrils flared as he gripped the steering wheel.

"Do you know what the fuck you just did?"

"He said never get less than six stacks."

"Carson practically got his Fredricko on his ass. He didn't need to know he was short. There's no such thing as short with him."

Brecee sat up and aided his bloody nose.

"What does that mean?"

Louie stared at Brecee with contempt, but it was soon replaced with an emotion Brecee was sure Louie didn't possess fear.

"Don't tell him it was Carson we saw tonight. I'll make it up to Carson. Just don't pull no stupid shit like that again. You got a question, ask me."

"Brecee, you've made me so proud," Fredricko announced with a lazy smile. Brecee snapped back to reality, noticing how

85

stiff Louie had gotten beside him. His eyes were swimming with that same fear from the night before.

Louie had taken over once they got back to the warehouse. He managed to slap on a goofy smile and patted Brecee on the shoulder.

"Our boy has made us a fortune. He's good after all."

"By who?"

"Some trust fund college kid," Louie lied with ease. He bumped Brecee on the shoulder with a glittering smile that was followed by a flash warning in his eyes.

"Show me the money then, Brecee," Fredricko ordered.

Brecee nervously opened the bag as if it containted the last contents of his soul. Lying to Fredricko was a death sentence.

Will he kill me for this?

Once Fredricko saw the stacks of money, he morphed into an excited kid. Brecee's memories kept merging together as he tried to make himself out to be the hero Fredricko was crowning him as.

The bumping music and gorgeous women only made him sick to his stomach.

"Look happy," Louie whispered as he sat close to Brecee. Brecee's breathing became staggered. The only window he could see from where he was seated had moonlight streaming into it. He thought back to the night he crashed on Zach's couch and the warning Zach kept giving him. Despite the money and high-rise place Fredricko gave him, he never felt emptier.

"It's not what I expected," Brecee said slowly.

"His reaction?"

"No. The money."

Louie turned to stare at Brecee. "There's no going back now. Don't think about Carson."

"What about my Ma? And my girl? Jordan?" Panic started to settle in.

Could he find Ma? Would he hurt Naudia?

Louie grabbed Brecee's wrist and held it tightly. It reminded Brecee the way his own dad would grab him when he'd throw a fit in public. His lips would curl into a tight, thin O shape and his words became a gritted command.

"It's too late for that shit," Louie grunted. Brecee looked at Louie in horror as he came to realize the hole he'd dug. Louie loosened his grip and forced a relaxed look on his face. The music became echoes in Brecee's ears as his heartbeat banged in his eardrums. He could feel the anxiety tighten in his chest.

"Whatever happens," Louie said quietly. "I won't let you sink."

Before Brecee could even react, there was a loud crash towards the front door. Suddenly, Fredricko's body was slammed across the floor and he flipped over the couch. Brecee hadn't even noticed Fredricko left the couch.

There were screams and women scattering to the corners as four men in identical black suits came walking in. They all had blank stares as they scanned the room. The one closest to Fredricko pulled out his gun and pointed it at his leg.

"Hold it, Brian," a smooth voice called. Brecee's heart stopped as he saw Carson glide into the room in a suit and tie. Carson scanned the room with a chilling smile. He took in the tall ceilings and flashing lights with a curious bitterness. His eyes eventually made it towards the other side of the room where Brecee and Louie sat. Fredricko and Brecee locked eyes and Brecee knew he was marked for death.

"What's the problem, Carson?" Louie asked coolly as he stood up slowly.

"Yeah, what is the problem?" Fredricko repeated. "I thought you said you used a trust fund kid." Fredricko's face was red with rage.

"Your new boy thought he was a tough shot. It seems you think I owe you something." Carson swiftly knelt down and grabbed Fredricko by the collar. He took a knife out of his pocket and held it against Fredricko's collar.

"I gave you everything," Carson spat. "How dare you."

"I don't know what he said but I swear to God I never meant to offend you." In a matter of seconds Fredricko turned into the

88

same person Brecee was when he was at his Ma's mercy. His eyes were bulged, and his lips chattered with fear.

He ain't free. He ain't no different from me.

Carson let Fredricko go and turned to walk away.

"I'll expect my fifty grand by tomorrow."

Before Carson even left the apartment Fredricko reached for his gun under the couch and aimed it for Brecee. Brecee froze as the bullet came for him.

I deserve it. I don't know why I was even born.

Louie pushed Brecee with superhuman strength allowing the bullet to hit him right in the chest. He felt to the floor with a loud thud. Brecee couldn't make sense of the screams and outpour of bullets. Fredricko aimed again for Brecee but he managed to slip through the side door and out onto the balcony.

The night air was cold against his skin, but he felt nothing. He climbed down the railing with ease, not even taking into account how far down he'd have to climb. Before he knew it, the screaming and gunshots were distant sounds high up, and he jumped down onto a dumpster.

His legs carried him faster than he knew he was even capable of. Tears streamed down his face as Louie's lifeless body stayed etched in his mind. All he could see was Ma's face crying and screaming at his funeral.

His lungs eventually gave out and he collapsed on the ground. A scream pierced the air and it took Brecee a few moments to realize it was his own. He had no idea how he had gotten so low.

Police sirens rang nearby but he didn't have the strength to run anymore. He reached into his pockets and pulled out the left-over cocaine pouches he had.

"I'm so sorry, Naudia. Ma."

"Brecee Monroe? Hello? Did you hear anything I just said?"

Brecee's eyes fluttered opened and adjusted to a dim-lit interrogation room. A dark-haired man with a receding hairline and dark undereye circles was sitting across from him. His wrists had cuffs around them, and he noticed he was wearing and orange jumpsuit.

Brecee moaned and tried to flinch and free himself.

"What the fuck? Where am I?"

The man sighed and took a sip of coffee.

"For the hundredth time you've been arrested for possession of drugs."

"Give him a break Johnson, he's coming off his high." Another man circled around Brecee. He was a tall Asian man with thick, hair, thin lips and huge teeth. His eyes were cold with not a hint of forgiveness.

He sat down slowly in the chair next to the other man without taking his eyes off Brecee.

"Listen, I can imagine this is really scary. You're in a strange place. You're chained up. Hell, you have no idea what's even occurred before you got in here."

"Like having the shit beat out of you."

"Johnson, please."

"Who beat me?" Brecee croaked.

"Let's start over. I'm Anthony and this is Larry."

Anthony smiled in an attempt to show a trace of friendliness but Brecee knew it was an act. Larry stood up and grabbed his coffee, sipping it slowly.

"Names are pointless. I want to know how you got to work for Fredricko."

Brecee's heart stopped as he remembered Louie's dead body.

"He's gonna kill my Ma—"

"He's on the run."

"You're lying."

"Nope. After the shootout he left with his posse."

"He owes Carson fifty grand," Brecee said.

"Not anymore," Anthony said with a shrug. "Carson's a dead man."

"How?"

"Why do you think Fredricko is on the run?" Larry asked. "He's got people coming after him."

None of it made sense to Brecee. How could Fredricko kill somehow as powerful as Carson?

"Last night they both tried to come for me. Fredricko killed Louie."

Anthony and Larry exchanged a glance followed by Larry sitting back down.

"Louis Michael was one of the most wanted drug dealers in the city. I'm sure it's a painful recollection that he's dead, but you're lucky it wasn't you."

"I should be dead. I put my entire family in danger."

"Your family is fine. If anything, they're more worried about you. The past month—"

"Month?"

The small room got colder and smaller. Brecee scanned the blank, gray walls and the faces of the two men before him. They couldn't care less about a thug like him. He knew that. But if Carson and Fredricko were dead, what was his life about to look like?

A tear fell down Brecee's cheek.

"My Ma was right," he whispered. "I really did end up just like my pops."

Larry grabbed a file from under the chair and opened it, sliding it across the table.

"It doesn't have to be a death sentence, kid. If you can remember the names of some of the men Fredricko was associated with, the judge is willing to bring your sentence down to three years."

Brecee knew that was stupid, though. Fredricko hated rats. As soon as Brecee got back out on the streets he'd take him out.

"I'm not a snitch."

"Think of your family, Brecee," Anthony said. "If Fredricko is still out there he can easily find your family."

"Or your little girlfriend," Larry said as he peaked at the open file. "A Naudia Vontane?"

Brecee kicked the table with his knees and tried to lunge at Larry but Anthony pulled a gun out.

"Don't do anything stupid. We're trying to help you."

"Fuck that. I don't trust y'all's kind. My daddy did and look what happened to him."

Anthony and Larry were silent.

"I know I got a bad record. But giving up names isn't what I do. I've been in this long enough to know how stupid that is."

"We know there's a lot at stake," Anthony said in a softer tone.

"Y'all don't know shit. You don't know what it's like to be where I'm at right now," Brecee's voice cracked. "I let everyone in my life down. Especially the person I loved most. And for what? To be uplifted by some punk-ass dealer who still kneeled down for someone above him."

Anthony tapped the file with a thin finger.

"That's why we need the names Brecee. You know what the cops found when they raided that apartment? A book about law. Something tells me this life can easily be switched around for something better."

The torn pages of the book fluttered behind Brecee's eyes. He could feel the thin, half torn pages on his fingertips.

"Has it really been a month or are y'all fucking with me?"

"You were higher than a kite when they picked you up. The detox has apparently been hard on you, not to mention solitary hasn't made much of a difference either," Larry explained.

"The psychiatrist believes it was a response to extreme grief which is expected when one gets arrested for a heavy charge."

Brecee eyed the file.

I'm in here. So it's over for me. I'ma have to let go of Naudia and ever living up to Ma's hopes and dreams.

All Brecee could remember about Naudia was the last time she kissed him. She had a worried glint in her eyes as she held his face in her small hands.

"You come back to me, alright?" she'd ordered. Brecee promised he would. But he was lying. He'd lied to every person in his life that he cared about. There wasn't much to look forward to.

"I'll tell y'all what you wanna know. Just make sure my people are taken care of."

CHAPTER ELEVEN

Brecee sold his life away in a matter of minutes. He told the detectives everything they needed to know and watched the smug looks on their faces as they wrote down details. Towards the end, they high-fived each other and mumbled about going for drinks afterwards, as they left Brecee handcuffed to the metal table. A corrections guard came in briskly and lifted Brecee up.

They walked him back to the hallway he came from but passed the tiny cell he had been staying in.

"Wait, am I moving?"

"You confessed. You're officially a criminal."

The life dragged out of Brecee's body as officers walked him to another huge, black door that read "C BLOCK." Once it was opened, the cries and yells of convicted felons and murderers filled the air. The cells weren't regular gates where you could peer inside at the criminal; they were huge, gray metal doors with only a small window on the door.

The officer unlocked a door and slung it open, throwing Brecee inside with one push.

"You'll see a judge in thirty days."

"Can I make a call—"

The door slid shut and Brecee was locked inside. There were whispers in the cells beside him but all Brecee could see was that cold look in Fredricko's eyes when he shot Louie dead.

Brecee crumbled to the floor and cried softly as he came to realize he truly was nothing.

"Aye, aye."

Brecee looked up to see an overweight Asian man with a tattoo on the left side of his face staring down at him. He was now in the community hall but forgot when he moved there.

"Am I in the way?"

"Nah, just wanted to see what you in for?"

Brecee sighed and poked at the lumpy mashed potatoes on his tray.

"Drugs."

"Doing or selling?"

"What you think?"

The man looked Brecee up and down and winched. "Shit. What are you, nineteen?"

"Twenty-six in February."

"Goddamn that's a shame."

Brecee nodded mechanically. If he had been on the outside, he probably would've asked why the man had a huge tattoo on his face or If he was born in New York. But the past couple of nights were all a blur that were stuck together in an endless loop. The wake-up calls, basketball court at noon, mandatory church sessions; it was never-ending. Brecee was just numb. He hadn't heard a word from Ma or Jordan. Naudia.

"Let me ask you something," the man said again after a painfully long silence. He kept looking over his shoulder as if someone was forcing him to ask.

"What?" Brecee asked dryly.

"You know somebody named Steven Monroe?"

Brecee's blood went cold. Everything turned to red as he stood up and threw his tray at the man. He started to reach for his neck to choke him, but the guard grabbed his arms and pulled them behind his back.

"That's a charge, Monroe! You want another fifteen years added?"

Brecee's skin crawled at the sound of fifteen.

"I don't wanna be here. I don't wanna fuckin' be here!" Brecee cried out. His voice sounded foreign to his ears as it filled the huge community room with piercing shrills that hit the top of the glass roof. He kicked and struggled and could feel the heat of rage and frustration kicking in.

"Leave my boy, now."

The guards stopped as If the voice of God had just spoken. All of the remaining chatter was muted as a tall, thin, dark skin man with a shiny bald head stood up. He was wearing the same prison clothes as everyone else but had a swagger to him. His shoulders were broad, and his arms toned with faded tattoos. Brecee's eyes bulged out of his head as he looked the man up and down. It was his dad.

"Sorry, Monroe, but this one gotta go back in." The guard spoke to Brecee's dad as if he was apologizing for doing his job. Not like he was speaking to a criminal who could easily end his life if he wanted to.

"I know Officer Mendes. Just be careful, that's my baby boy right there."

Brecee hated his dad for so long but was filled with nostalgia at the sound of his voice. The way he'd gloss over his words smoothly and make the most boring things sound interesting.

Steven stood and watched the guards drag Brecee back to his room with a faint smile on his face. If Brecee hadn't spent half his life wishing his dad were dead, he knew he would have run to him and hugged him.

Brecee was placed in solitary for the rest of the day. He stared at the padded walls and went in between sleep and waking up with cold sweat all over his body. He lost track of the day and was afraid they'd leave him in there to die.

But before he knew it, the door was opened and bright, morning light came streaming in. A female officer was standing by the door with a friendly but stern look.

"Go on and get up now. I hope you learned your lesson," she said in a thick, Louisiana accent. "We don't take kindly to that fighting shit."

Brecee stood up and walked out the door like a feeble child.

"It won't happen again, lady."

"Officer Lisa."

Brecee winced as he repeated, "Officer Lisa."

She took him back to the same community room where all the prisoners stared in awe at him.

"I gotta say it's not every day we get fathers and sons in here. Your daddy is respected here, so I'm sure you'll be just fine."

Officer Lisa patted Brecee on the shoulder and swiftly walked away, leaving him in the middle of the room with curious eyes taking him in.

"Brecee. Over here."

Steven was waving his arm at a small table by the door. There were four other huge men with rough scars and tattoos on their faces. Once Brecee approached the table they all got up in unison.

One of the men, a muscular white man with a scar on his head, held his hand out.

"Heard so much 'bout you. Glad to finally meet you."

Brecee shook his hand slowly then sat down in front of Steven.

"I'll see y'all in the court soon."

Steven turned to Brecee with a huge smile. He reached across the table to shake Brecee's hand, but Brecee recoiled.

"Why the fuck you trying to touch me?"

"Ah, so you still mad."

"Grew up without you like every other black kid. What you think?"

Steven tapped his long fingers on the table with a sympathetic look on his face.

"It'll always be the biggest regret of my life. Leaving your Ma and Jordan and you behind. But now I have another regret. Seeing you here."

"It's my life don't worry 'bout it."

"You still my son, boy. I wrote you so many letters and begged your Ma to bring you here."

Brecee laughed at the thought of Ma following the instructions of anyone.

"You chose the wrong woman to be expecting favors like that."

Steven chucked. "Your Ma was a difficult but amazing woman."

"Then why you leave her?"

Steven sighed, rubbing his hand over his head. He stared down at the table trying to recall all the small moments of his life that led to him being torn away from his family.

"It wasn't my plan," Steven said softly. "Your Ma was struggling so much at the hospital and certain bills weren't getting paid. I promised her I wouldn't deal no more, but she never believed me. She knew I wasn't shit."

Brecee felt a pang in his chest as he thought back to all the conversations, he had with Naudia about Ma and Jordan not thinking he was shit.

Is that why Ma kept trying to get Naudia to leave? So, she wouldn't end up like Ma?

"Eventually, I got caught up with the wrong folks and had to pay the price. Just like you."

Brecee lifted his gaze to finally look into his dad's eyes. All he saw was himself. The years of torment and trying to get it right; people not believing in him and hating him.

"Ma always said I'd be just like you. So, I figured if I hated you it would lessen the chance."

Steven reached across the table again to squeeze Brecee's hand. Brecee didn't flinch and instead allowed himself to feel the roughness of his dad's fingers. The familiarity of the dark marks on his knuckles and the tiny scar by his thumb he got after freeing Brecee's arm from the washer when he was four.

"I ain't blaming her or you son. I know y'all both had it rough."

Words refused to form as the pain hit Brecee's chest. He felt it in waves the first couple of weeks, but as he sat there finally holding his dad's hand and accepting that Ma, Jordan, and Naudia would never be in his life again, the pain was despicable.

Steven got up and hurried to the other side of the table to hug brecee. Brecee let himself revert back to the same little boy who cried until his throat was sore, when Steven was put into a cop car. The anger was replaced with grief.

"I fucked my life up. I don't deserve to live," Brecee wailed. Steven pulled Brecee away and shook him.

"Don't you ever say no shit like that again, you hear? Your life is nowhere near over. You fucked up but you still got a chance."

"When I first got in here, they said fifteen years."

"You met with the judge after you talked to the detectives?"

Brecee shook his head.

"Then you got time. How many days did they say?"

"Thirty."

Steven pursed his lips and patted Brecee roughly on the back.

"It's gonna be a fight but there is a sure for hell way to get you out, son. I just need you to trust me."

Chapter Twelve

Julie Monroe refused to get out of bed to face the world. Her body felt limp and weak and the day melted into the night quicker than usual. She'd hear Jordan rattling around downstairs, making urgent calls, and the muffled cries at night. It was painful to lose a brother, but it wouldn't compare to losing two children.

Jordan knocked lightly on the door and eased into the bedroom.

"Ma, it's six o' clock and you didn't touch the sandwich I left," Jordan said as he noticed the uneaten sandwich by the bedstand. "Doc says you gotta keep your strength."

"How can I, Jordan? It's too much."

Jordan sat on the end of the bed like he used to when he was younger. The first time Brecee had a run in with the cops Ma let him spend the night in jail. She cried the entire night and Jordan came in and out of the room. He'd stay quiet and just listen to the rise and fall of Ma's cries until eventually she fell asleep.

"I know you're hurting, Ma. I am, too."

"Not as much as me, Jordan. I didn't do enough for you two."

Jordan crawled on the bed and laid next to Ma, holding her hand.

"You're the most beautiful and strongest woman I have ever known. How could you say that?"

"Because," Julie started to say. She stopped as a lump formed in her throat.

"Jordan, I hate him. I've hated him for years for all the stress, but most of all because he was so much like his daddy."

The words hit the stale air like smoke. It hung there as the intensity of Ma's statement filled Jordan's heart with confusion and relief. He would never wish harm on Brecee, but he also hated him for being hard-headed and putting Ma through so much.

"He was lost but it was never an excuse to be so damn selfish," Jordan said. "Don't feel bad about feeling that way. Most people would have cut him off years ago."

Julie sat up and reached for the sandwich. The bread was dry, but it was something to put on her stomach.

"And Naudia? Does she know?"

"Of course. Her parents, too. They were trying to find something to sue Brecee on, but I convinced him his sentence would be long enough."

Julie took another bite of the sandwich then set it back down on the side table.

"I feel sorry for her but it's better now than years after she's settled down with Brecee and had kids," Julie said with a blank stare. Jordan leaned in and kissed her on the cheek.

"I know, Ma. I know."

Naudia sat in a brand-new Chanel suit as she waited for her parents to finish talking with the detectives. They all agreed to meet at her dad's office on the nineteenth floor to discuss "details." Her mother purposefully left out the real intentions in an effort not to alarm Naudia. It was too late, though; Naudia already heard the news. She saw all the Instagram posts and interviews on television. Brecee had actually gone down for the biggest drug bust in their neighborhood.

When her mother brought the Chanel suit that was still in its hanging bag, she also had a fresh coffee in her other hand. She laid the hanging bag on Naudia's bed and handed her the coffee.

"You'll never guess who gave you first serve on the latest suit," she mused as she unzipped the bag. It was a cream blazer with a matching skirt with emerald trimmings on the sleeves. Naudia shrugged and took a sip of her coffee. The suit was all for publicity. Her mother's socialite friends were buzzing with the drama and she needed a way to showcase that her only daughter was still pretty and acceptable despite her poor habits.

"It's pretty," Naudia said flatly. She looked over at her mother as she forced herself to blink back tears. Her stomach felt like it was doing back flips. Her parents were actually right. Brecee lied to her time and time again and was a felon.

The only guy that truly loved me was a felon.

Naudia watched her mother blab on about the suit and the new shoes she bought for Naudia. She watched her mother light up at the topic of everything besides the heartache Naudia was experiencing.

Is that who I have to become to avoid being the dumb girl who gets lied to?

Naudia didn't want to be the woman who obsessed over materialistic things like suits or marry a man who couldn't decide which day he'd love her. However, she faced the fact that she was no different than her mother because Brecee broke her heart.

"Mom?"

"Yes, sweetheart?"

"Will I ever move on from this? Will I ever be normal?" The words hurt to say. Naudia's mom kissed her gently on the forehead.

"Yes, you will. You walk into the office tomorrow with your head high. You did nothing wrong."

The morning went by fast, too. Before Naudia knew it, she was passing wide-eyed faces with polite smiles. She walked wedged in between her parents and for once felt safe. Her dad was many things but when it came to his family, he considered their well-being a priority.

The private detectives, Anthony and Larry, were shabby looking men with five'o clock shadows. Anthony was more talkative and had a small mouth with huge teeth. Larry had a stern face with a balding head and square jaw.

"Miss Vontane," they sang in unison. Naudia nodded and walked into the office.

"Let's make this quick. I have a fundraiser to get to," Naudia said. She could hear her mother speaking through her. It was too late to turn back now.

They sat around Naudia and pulled out a small note pad.

"How long did you and Brecee Monroe date?"

"Two years."

"Did he ever talk about his work?"

"No. He told me he worked at a warehouse which we all know was a lie."

Naudia could see her parents sitting outside the glass doors of the office with satisfied smiles on their faces. She wondered if they were happy Brecee was rotting behind bars. If they preferred her to blossom into a heartless, quick-tongued creature to avoid heartbreak.

"Our records show he purchased several items with his drug earned money, including a diamond bracelet for you."

"Yes, it's been handed over to the authorities." Naudia's mother had to hold her in an iron hold as her dad took the bracelet off her wrist. Even if it was just an item, it was the last thing Brecee ever gave her.

"Wow looks like you've done everything by the book," Anthony said in awe.

"I expect nothing else from the daughter of Mister Vontane," Larry said. "He's royalty down here."

Naudia hesitated as her initial knee-jerk reaction would be to insult her dad's reputation. Instead, her body felt numb and she felt her old self die in that very moment.

"Yes, he is truly an inspiration. I'm lucky to have him as a father."

After the questioning, Naudia followed her parents out of the office and into their limo. She stared out the window as they drove through the neighborhood, passing the familiar streets where she and Brecee fell in love.

"You're going to love the beach house in Honolulu, sweetie," Naudia's mom chirped from the front. The noise of her mother explaining a new line of shoes to her father as he grunted here and there, all blending together. Naudia wiped the last tears away as she said her final goodbye to Brecee Monroe. She knew she'd never see him again. Not with the life she was entering.

I'll always love you, no matter what.

CHAPTER THIRTEEN

B recee and Steven spent every single day together, whether they were eating lunch or working out in the courtyard. He was the cream of the crop in the prison hierarchy, and Steven was to thank.

Ever since Steven first landed in prison, he had to assert his dominance and claim territory. There were several gangs that either wanted to kill Steven or make him a part of their crew.

"I stayed solo for a minute, though. Even when the Puerto Ricans and Koreans promised to cut my throat in my sleep. They were mad I got out so easy," Steven explained as Brecee ate a stale piece of bread.

"Off easy? You serving a life sentence, pops."

"They woulda preferred me dead. I had too much information on me to be walking alive. It took five years of always looking over my shoulder before I finally got peace in this place," Steven said with a sigh. Brecee noticed the lines along his face that likely came from the years of stress and worrying if that night would be his last.

"How'd you get peace?"

"Made a deal with my enemy's enemy," Steven said with a smile. "It was a gamble. I could've gotten myself gutted like a damn fish. But it worked out. His folks on the outside took care of him. Since I gained their trust, I got respect from everyone in here."

A group of Korean men with sleeve tattoos walked by Steven and Brecee. One of them placed two orange juices on the table then followed behind the others.

"Wait, you with the Koreans, pops?"

Steven laughed and opened the orange juice.

"Their lead man was the one who saved my ass. But I got peace with every crew. I stay out of their shit and mind my damn business. Something you gotta do, too."

Steven handed Brecee the opened juice.

"Who was it you was working for?"

Brecee took a long sip, not wanting to reveal the name. It tasted like poison to him because if it weren't for Fredricko, he could've been on the outside living with Naudia.

"Fredricko-"

Steven slammed his fist on the table and groaned.

"Shit, Brecee!"

"What?"

113

"I already know who you talking about."

"You know Fredricko?"

"A few years before I was arrested, he was just starting to work his way in. He was a greedy one, too."

"He worked for a Carson-"

"O'Reilly. Yeah, yeah. That was a cold man, too. I can't believe you got involved with the folks I was too scared to even look at."

Brecee was stunned to hear his father talk about being fearful of Fredricko. Aside from the bullet he put in Louie's chest, Fredricko had been a father figure to Brecee.

"He took care of me when I was at my lowest."

"By feeding you coke and making you do his dirty work?"

"How did you know about that?"

"It ain't hard to tell when you been in here for so long. Also, a couple of people saw them drag your high ass in twitching and screaming."

Brecee had no memory of what it was like when he first arrived, but he figured it wasn't pretty. He had scars on his arms from where he scratched and bit himself when they forced him to detox.

"Well, I'll see what this judge says about all this."

"I hope they're easier on you than they were with me."

"What happened with that? Why they do that to you?"

Steven stared straight ahead at the double doors, unable to answer Brecee's question. After all the years he spent locked up, even he didn't have the answers. He cried and screamed himself to sleep so many times that it was better for him not to even try and crack his own case.

"It don't matter, son. I ain't getting out and I wouldn't want to. This here is my life and I'm okay with that."

A correction officer walked up to Steven with a sour expression.

"Your requested visit expires in thirty minutes, Steven."

"Who you visiting with?" Brecee asked. Steven stood up and started to walk away.

"Just my psychologist. Nothing special, son."

The visiting area was full of hushed voices and yearning faces behind the glass window. Steven walked to the end of the room where a single chair with a black phone waited for him. He braced himself as he sat down and picked up the phone.

"Hi, Jules."

Julie Monroe sat behind the glass with half frown, half smile. She hated Steven but knew she'd always have love for him.

"Hello, Steven. You seen our boy?"

"Unfortunately. He's good, though."

"Wouldn't be in here if it weren't for you."

Steven gritted his teeth. Julie would never forgive him for abandoning her after all the years that passed.

"It is on my conscience, Julie. But that's not no eight-year-old lil boy back there. He's grown and is in control of his own decisions."

Julie slapped the glass with the palm of her hand.

"My son is facing a life sentence and you think this is just something he gotta hold?"

Steven lowered his head as curious eyes stared them down.

"Julie, I don't mean it like that. But I don't want him to hold his head down and think he's just a loser for the rest of his life."

"Well he is and always has been cause he's just like you."

"Listen here," Steven said through gritted teeth. "I fucked up and hurt you. It's fine if you hate me, but don't you dare put that on Brecee. You're a strong, smart woman. You raised them the best you could, and I thank you for that."

Julie looked away with tears in her eyes.

"I'll never forgive you, Steven. You know, that right?"

Steven stared at Julie through the glass with regret in his heart. He loved her deeper than anyone. When they were young, he promised he'd give her the life she deserved. He was too greedy to see how his dealing would tear them apart.

"I do. But now it's time for me to help my son for once. Did you get the file I asked for?"

Julie nodded and pulled out a folder from her purse.

"I'll send it through the front desk." Julie got up with her purse on her shoulder.

"Will you see Brecee?"

"I don't ever want to see him again. But I do hope he gets out. And know that I love him."

Julie hung the phone up and walked out of the visiting room. Steven covered his face with his hand to hide the tears that he couldn't stop from streaming down his cheeks

It was two weeks until Brecee got to see the judge. Each day brought more fear and anxiety, especially with the occasional news reports he'd hear on the TV in the community room.

"Brecee Monroe, the twenty-five-year-old drug dealer, was arrested and will be charged with possession of drugs as well as the murder of Louis Williams."

Before Brecee could even panic, Steven pulled him out of the room.

"Don't listen to that, son."

"They putting Louie's murder on me? I would never murder anyone!" Brecee's voice cracked.

"You gotta stay cool, alright?" Steven urged. He pulled a yellow folder out of his pants and placed it in Brecee's hands. "This right here is your ticket."

Brecee took the folder and opened it. It had several pages of reports and pictures of Fredricko.

"What is this, pops? You making a case against Fredricko?"

"That right there is your proof of innocence son. Don't worry about how I got it. Just know this and your confession against Fredricko will clear your name. That's why your sentence was long in the first place."

Steven leaned his back against the wall and took the folder back from Brecee.

"Took a good year's worth of commissary, but it's worth it. That private detective owed me anyways."

Brecee's chest felt lighter. It amazed him how he had only been in prison for a short while, yet his dad already made sacrifices. Ma made many sacrifices but towards the end she got tired of looking out for Brecee.

"I was thinking of calling Ma or Jordan, but the last time I tried they wouldn't pick up," Brecee said softly.

"Son," Steven said with a tinge of sadness in his tone. "You will never be the same after this. Your folks on the outside will never look at you the same. Not even your ma."

A lump formed in Brecee's throat at the thought of getting out and being ignored completely.

"I'm her son, Pops. She can't really hate me like that."

Steven stared straight ahead with his lips pursed in deep thought. Brecee knew he spent years trying to reconcile with Ma, but after a while he likely gave up. Ma never stopped talking down on him, either. Brecee knew she was a good woman who just wanted the best for her family. Even after the rejection and loneliness he felt, he knew he'd never hate her for giving up.

"Your Ma is a dynamic woman, but she feels everything. She's a mother. A wife. She just wanted love and lost her first son, and then the youngest ends up in prison. She's tired, son. It's hard to accept but you have to let her go."

The light in the hallway seemed to blind Brecee as he tried to push his pain further down. It haunted him to know the possibility of him never seeing the daylight outside of prison windows again. The smell of generic mop water and discarded bits of lumpy meatloaf were the new smells that Brecee had to endure. For the first time in his life, though, he wasn't blaming anyone for where he was.

"You right, Pops. They tried to warn me, but I didn't listen. I was so caught up in trying to prove I was something that they could be proud of," Brecee admitted quietly. "I just couldn't get myself out that hole of feeling sorry for myself."

"Sounds a lot like me when I was your age," Steven said with a wistful expression. "I was so bent on letting everyone know how much my life sucked and how it was their fault. But they didn't put me in here, Brecee. My actions did. Your actions put you in here."

The truth stung but it was still gentle. As Brecee looked at Steven's profile he was reminded of Louie and the way he talked about his own son. Louie's eyes were full of torment.

"I don't wanna die in that lifestyle," Brecee said. Steven reached his arm over Brecee's shoulders and squeezed.

"You won't, son. I know your ma has been hard on you these years and maybe said things that hurt your ego. But I see you, Brecee. Always have, even when you refused to talk to me."

Brecee thought back to the drawer at Ma's house full of letters from his dad. Each envelop was worn with different stickers that changed from bumblebees and superman to a plain purple heart. The letters were filled to the brim, yet back then, Brecee hated to see them. As he stood against the wall with his dad's arm wrapped over his shoulder, he wondered what the letters talked about and if he had read them would his life have turned out differently.

The questions were blinding to Brecee, just like the light streaming in the three, huge windows in the hallway. The sun was starting to fade and cast an orangey-yellow glow into the hallway. Despite not knowing what was to come, Brecee felt loved and safe.

"Pops?"

"Yeah?"

"I love you," Brecee said. "I'm sorry for hating you all these years."

Steven smiled and kissed Brecee on the forehead.

"You don't even have to say it for me to know."

There was warmth between Steven and Brecee that mended the brokenness Brecee swore would stay with him until the day he died.

CHAPTER FOURTEEN

The streets felt eerily bare without Brecee by his side. Zach spent his days staying low and making deals here and there. He swore he'd be the one who'd get caught up and arrested since Brecee was much more careful than he was.

Except in the end, it was his best friend who got the heat. The thought of Brecee being locked up in a small cell with hundreds of violent men made Zach lose sleep at night.

Apart from the nightmares, Zach had been watching his back out of fear for Fredricko. It was news on the streets that he was out for blood when the word got out that Brecee's sentence could be shortened if he gave up names. He had smartened up since the last time he dealt with Brecee, he was careless with no worries. It was no longer a game anymore.

"That nigga a snitch," Marco, one of Zach's part time dealers said as they sat on the curb in front of Zach's apartment. Marco was nothing like Brecee; he was sloppy and didn't care what people thought of him. Even though Brecee cared so much about what his Ma and brother thought, he made a great business partner.

"You tellin' me you'd spend a lifetime in prison for a nigga that killed one of your boys?"

Marco shrugged and chugged his beer down. He was covered in sweat and potato skin flakes.

"I ain't dumb enough to get caught. Kid was messin with Fredricko of all dealers," Marco said. He belched loudly and leaned his back against the hot curb. "Best just to stay low."

"Brecee wasn't like that, though. He was smart. I never understood why he got in the dealing game in the first place," Zach said with his elbows resting on his knees. "We was boys."

Brecee taught Zach so much. He thought about visiting Brecee when he first got arrested, but his main man, Shaneal, promised to beat him black and blue if he was seen with Brecee. Brecee was a cancer in the dealing world, and if Zach wanted to keep his family safe, he'd have to keep his distance.

Besides, he'd already been visited by the two detectives to know he better be smart.

"Did you all deal together?" Larry asked. Larry and Anthony cornered Zach at his day job serving drinks at the local bar. As soon as they walked into the bar with their button ups and corporate ties, Zach knew what was going on.

"Nope. I don't deal. I work at the bar."

Larry laughed and leaned forward. His face was red and pudgy, and he had an arrogant air about him.

"You expect me to believe that? What's that saying Anthony? Birds of a feather flock together?"

Anthony snorted and folded his arms across his chest. Zach smirked and looked them both up and down. He could easily take them both out in their secondhand suit jackets.

"Y'all think you can come in this neighborhood and demand answers and shit? I told you what I know. That's it. Brecee was my boy and I'm praying to God he gets off this damn murder charge."

Zach's chest felt tight when he thought back to Brecee's anxiety of almost getting caught.

"Okay, okay. I suppose we believe you," Anthony said. "But did you know Fredricko?"

Zach shrugged. "Never heard of him."

They knew he was lying. They could tell from the tattoos underneath his sheer button up, and the roughness of his knuckles. But they weren't here to convict Zach of a crime they couldn't show evidence for.

Zach watched them walk out of the bar like a pair of bulldogs.

"Fucking pigs," he muttered under his breath.

"Mister Monroe?"

Jordan looked up at the several faces staring at him in his board meeting. He cleared his throat and sat up straight. He called all of his colleques for assistance in putting together a team for Brecee's case.

"Uh, yes?"

"Are you sure you want to offer the help of an attorney to, ah, Brecee Monroe?" She said his name like he was a stranger. Like Jordan had just heard about him from the news and decided to help his case.

"My brother?" Jordan said with annoyance. "Of course. Just make sure the tip is anonymous. I need to make sure he has the best-case scenario."

"I think he has a really good case, Jordan," Gretchen Leigh whispered in Jordan's ear. They'd been mutual friends of the firm since their grad school days when Jordan would spend hours going over case files with her. Gretchen was aware of the strain Brecee's case had on him.

"Thank you, I just hope this helps him."

The rest of the team muttered their polite goodbyes and headed out the door. Jordan remained seated and looked out the window.

"What's on your mind?" Gretchen asked softly. She was decently pretty with a small face and short blond hair. Despite Brecee's suspicions, white women weren't Jordan's first choice.

Relationships period were never on his radar with the stress of caring for Ma.

"My younger brother is in prison and there's a possibility he'll never get out. I don't know if I'd ever speak to him again," Jordan said in one breath. He exhaled sharply as the pain rested on his chest.

Gretchen placed her hand over Jordan's and leaned in close to him so that her hair brushed against his cheek.

"I know this is heart breaking. But you've done all you can for him. Plus, you never know what the future brings."

Jordan nodded and slowly moved his hand away from Gretchen. It was a reaction that was cold on his part, but he felt too numb to even allow himself to open up to someone. Gretchen seemed to sense this and grabbed his forearm before he could make a swift exit.

"I care about you, Jordan. I always have. I'm not looking for anything crazy. Just let me be there for you."

As unnatural as it felt to be vulnerable in the midst of such heavy times, Jordan saw hope in Gretchen. He leaned over and kissed her softly on the cheek.

"Let's just hope for the best." The next day would determine everything. Regardless if Brecee got time knocked off his case, Jordan was ending the road of having Brecee in his life. It was the only way he could move on with his life without the nagging torment that Brecee was destroying his life.

It tore at Jordan. It made him want to take Brecee and shake him and scream in his face.

Why'd you have to be so damn stupid? Why didn't you listen?

Silent tears streamed down Jordan's cheeks, but he let them stay. There was no use in hiding his grief.

CHAPTER FIFTEEN

The courtroom was packed with news reporter and anxious eyes as Brecee was walked inside. He was given a fresh suit and pair of shoes to face the judge. Thanks to Steven, Brecee had a sharp attorney who made sure every corner was cut to ensure Brecee got what he needed.

They met twice before the court hearing in visitation. He was a short black man with a receding hairline and thick, brown glasses. His nose was short, and his ears stuck out. If Brecee hadn't known him, he was sure he'd laugh at his weird face and even weirder taste of burgundy suits.

"Marshall Jones," he said in a surprisingly deep voice. Brecee noticed the tan briefcase he set on the table that matched his coat perfectly.

"You a sharp-ass nigga," Brecee said in astonishment.

"Mister Monroe, I do not adhere to that kind of language, and for the sake of your trial, I suggest you don't either," Marshall replied sharply. "You need to be an angel in the eyes of the judge."

"My fault. I'm not used to ni-, uh, men like you," Brecee admitted politely. It was the truth, too. Aside from Jordan, most guys in the neighborhood would size you up and diminish you to the size of your place, then figure out who you were as a person.

"No need to apologize. We're not so different. We just have to present ourselves well to make sure you're given the correct sentencing."

Brecee allowed Marshall to take over. He listened to the way his voice would stay in a monotone wave, adding no emotional shrills the way Brecee's did. He also kept his face neutral, not worried if Brecee liked what he said. It was a talent in Brecee's eyes because every word he spoke was usually with insecurity.

Marshall went over the details of the case as well as drilled Brecee on what to say and how to act.

"Do not react angrily. No matter what the opposing side says. You have got to keep your cool, Brecee."

"So, be like you?"

Marshall smiled for the first time with small, gapped teeth.

"No, be like Brecee. From what I've been told you were actually on the debate team back in high school."

A warmth rinsed over Brecee as Marshall smiled at him. The debate team was a memory Brecee forced to the back of his mind. It was locked away and gathered dust for so long; Brecee couldn't stand to remember. Remembering the good things he did made the present hurt even more.

However, he finally allowed the memory of him sitting beside the smartest kids in school and sounding off his thoughts eloquently to penetrate his mind.

People were shocked since Brecee didn't do very well in any other class.

"I was alright. I really enjoyed it, though."

"Have you thought about life after prison?"

"No. I don't have anything—" Brecee paused, remembering the words his dad spoke to him. "Excuse me. I'm not sure what path to choose next."

Marshall grinned and reached into his briefcase and pulled out Brecee's beloved, tattered book. Brecee slapped his hand on the glass in desperation.

"How did you get that? I left it... I—"

"Let's just say someone felt you should have it. It was your saving grace. I can tell by the dog-eared pages and notes you scribbled."

"Who gave it to you?"

Marshall looked down at the book and sighed.

"I was told not to tell for your own sake. But Brecee, please know that there's people who care about you. People who want you to win."

Marshall placed the book against the glass so that Brecee was face to face with his only liberty.

"This is your next path, Brecee. And it's possible, too. They've got classes here. Take advantage of it."

As Brecee stood in front of the judge, he almost forgot where he was. He kept reliving the small moments where he messed his life up. When he fell in love with the most beautiful girl in Manhattan. When he broke his Ma's heart.

"Brecee Alexander Monroe," the judge said sternly. "Why shouldn't you spend the rest of your days in prison?"

The case made against Brecee was strong, but his side was even better. He knew he had the chance to prove himself and become the good man he was destined to be.

"Your honor, I was young and made poor decisions. I fully accept the damage I caused. I was raised by a strong woman who taught me right from wrong, but I got lost. I couldn't see who I was. I know that being in the real world will give me a chance to help people like me who grew up alone with a high chance of being in the system."

The judge nodded slowly. The remaining thirty minutes were used for closing arguments from tired-eyed attorneys, until the judge reached his final verdict.

"On the account of the presented evidence, it's clear that Brecee Monroe was involved in drugs. However, he worked with investigators and has promised to be a good citizen when he returns to society. I hereby sentence you to one year in state prison."

There were cheers in the courtyard and arms that wrapped tightly around Brecee. He felt none of it, though. He was high. He looked to the ceiling as his vision became blurred.

Thank you, God. I'm gonna be good. I'm gonna actually do good.

Through the overjoyed hugging bodies of his defense team, Brecee saw Ma and Jordan quietly leave the courtroom. He saw Ma's hair pulled back into a tight bun and Jordan's slender frame. They walked hand and hand as the double doors opened then closed.

I'll always love y'all. Be well. Take care, Ma and Jordan.

Steven was waiting in the community room anxiously. All his efforts the past month had gone into making sure Brecee was taken care of. It was something he sadly never got for his own case. All those years back, he was positive he'd get off since he was innocent. However, the detectives built a case so strong against him, he didn't stand a chance in the court room.

He figured his life was better in prison anyways. Seventeen years of imprisonment changed him completely. He got used to the blank taste of cafeteria food and trading an orange juice for cranberry. Toothpaste was just as valuable as holeless socks, and there was always the need of weapons to store in the mattress.

Since he was protected by the Korean gang, they gave him all types of special treatment. Loyalty was a huge thread for every man in prison because no matter how long the sentence, reputation on the outside could affect you behind bars.

"You think he got off?" Ryeo, a fellow Korean gangster asked as he sat down next to Steven. Ryeo came from a family full of murderers and dealers and he was serving forty years to life for taking out four brothers of an enemy gang. It seemed he knew prison was his future because he never moped or reminisced about the outside life. Like Steven, he found simple pleasures in his limited freedom.

"Not completely off, but I'm praying it won't be as long as mine," Steven said slowly. He was hunched over with his hands clasped together to take pressure off of his chest. Whenever difficult things happened, Steven's chest would close up and he'd feel like he was drowning. He had to keep himself sane for the sake of Brecee.

"Hope so," Ryeo said with a sigh. "He's a good kid. Smart, too. I heard him talking to Myron about the law and shit."

Steven grinned. "Yeah, you know he was on the debate team in high school? His Ma told me back when she used to write me. She sent me a picture." Steven dug in his pocket and took out a worn picture of fifteen-year-old Brecee with a goofy smile as he stood on a small stage with a silver trophy.

"My other son, Jordan, was the one people liked to uplift cause he had the grades. But I knew Brecee was just as good."

"What about the other one? Has he visited?"

"Nah. We got an understanding. He wants nothing to do with me or this prison."

Ryeo raised his eyebrows with a surprised look on his full face.

"Crazy how family's react to shit, right? My *appa* completely disowned me. Says he has two sons and one daughter now," Ryeo said. He smacked his lips and stared down at his meaty fingers that were caked with dirt.

"Can't blame 'em. We'll never know how much it hurts them," Steven reminded him. It took him close to fifteen years to fully understand and accept what follows a prison sentence.

"Well, your son is lucky to have you. Most of these assholes in here can't say their dad did half of the shit you have." Ryeo patted Steven on the back and left the community room for his cell. The clock ticked on until it eventually reached two o' clock. The huge double doors leading to the outside unlocked and then opened. Bright sunlight poured in as officers walked Brecee inside.

His head was down but he had a smile on his face.

"Brecee!" Steven called. The officers stopped and let Brecee wave at Steven.

"I got a year, Pops!"

Steven ran over to Brecee like lightning. The officers didn't bother to stop him. He held Brecee tightly and kissed him on the forehead.

"I'm so proud of you, boy. I'm so proud."

The officers pulled the two away and Steven had to contain his excitement. The other inmates started to clap with misty eyes, an effort Steven never thought he'd see.

"Yo, Steven," Carmello Williams, a notorious drug dealer and enemy of Steven's, called out. "I'm happy your boy got out."

It was a strange interaction, but Steven chose not to dwell on it. Most inmates would jump others with light sentences or try to get more time put on their agenda just for pure enjoyment.

"I appreciate that, Carmello."

Steven walked back to his cell with his shoulders back and head high. The following year was going to be him staying on Brecee's ass to make sure he did what he was supposed to.

Later on, Steven visited Brecee's cell and law books and pamphlets spread on his bunk.

"So, you really going back?"

"I got to Pops. I gotta do something with this freedom I've been given."

Steven sat next to Brecee. "Then I better not see you slacking off, you hear? I don't care if you got bad days. You better get this degree and be ready to get a job on the outside."

Brecee nodded with his favorite book in his lap.

"Ever since you got arrested, I wanted to go into being a lawyer."

"Like Jordan?" Steven snorted.

"Nah. Jordan don't care about prison shit. I wanna be the type that helps dudes like you out."

Steven stood up briskly and started to pace. "Don't waste your time on that, Brecee. I'm fine living in here-"

"I'm not. Especially when you're innocent. You said so yourself you didn't kill that man."

Steven was speechless. He wasn't sure if he should tell Brecee everything that was running through his head. There was much more to the story. So many fine details that Steven promised himself he'd take to the grave. But he never counted on his son to find him in prison. Now that Brecee's life had a chance to change for the better, Steven had to make the final decision and give him the truth.

"Maybe some other time we'll talk about it."

Steven quickly left Brecee's cell.

CHAPTER SIXTEEN

The prison's degree program was new and targeted at inmates with sentences under ten years. Brecee's first day in class was nerve-racking. School wasn't his strongest area and he had a tendency to slack off.

He pushed himself the way his dad expected him to and fought through moments of doubt. The instructor was an older black woman with short, platinum hair and one gold tooth. She'd circle around the room with her clipboard and occasionally lean over Brecee to help him with certain questions. She smelled like lavender and her necklace would always brush the back of Brecee's neck.

As Brecee was immersed in his work, he didn't care to notice the pair of eyes that were on him the moment he stepped into the class.

"You the one named Monroe?" he asked in a thick, Cuban accent. Brecee tore his eyes away from his computer.

"Brecee."

"Dominic."

Brecee gave Dominic a small finger wave and went back to his work. Dominic slid his chair over to Brecee so that they were deathly close. Brecee could smell a familiar scent of coconut and hair gel. Dominic had long, thin curly hair and a hooked nose. His skin was a soft brown with red undertones and when he grinned at Brecee's disgust of him moving closer, Brecee noticed his black and browning teeth.

"You and I aren't so different," Dominic whispered. "I'm getting out soon, too."

"Glad to hear that. But I don't think either one of us will get anything done if—"

"Your poppa is Steven Monroe, yes?"

The question was technically innocent. Brecee and Steven looked very similar and everyone around the prison pretty much knew how protective Steven was over Brecee. However, Dominic had a mischievous glint in his eye that made the hairs on the back of Brecee's neck stand up.

"Who's asking?"

Dominic licked his cracked lips over and over again.

"You must not recognize me, chico," he said in a low voice. Brecee folded his arms across his chest to hide the growing tension.

"Guess not, chico," Brecee replied.

"Do you know my tio? Fredricko?"

Suddenly, the small classroom became a war zone. Brecee no longer was flying from the high of his win where getting his degree and leaving prison were his only tasks. He was face to face to the bloodline of the man who he ratted out. Things were no longer simple.

"I know of him."

"Don't play coy," Dominic spat with his fingers gripping on the edges of the table. The blood drained from his face and his thin lips curled into a snarl exactly like Fredricko's did when he was furious.

"What do you want?"

"You're a rat, Brecee. You don't have one thread of honor."

Brecee grabbed Dominic by the color and brought Dominic close enough so he could smell the potato skins on his breath.

"Keep my name out your mouth. I don't know who got you up to this shit, but I'm definitely not the one."

"Is that so?" Dominic lifted his foot up and grabbed a sharped toothbrush. In a matter of seconds, he swung it at Brecee's throat, but Brecee ducked and kicked Dominic back. Brecee started for the door right when Brecee dug the sharpened toothbrush into his thigh. Brecee let out a blood curdling scream that sent the instructor running for the guard.

"You ain't never felt pain before, bitch," Dominic snarled. Dominic crawled to Brecee's stomach and was about to stab him, but he was grabbed by a short, Asian guy with a tattoo on his left cheek. Brecee didn't know his name but he recognized the tattoo from the Korean gang.

The guards rushed in and handcuffed Dominic.

"They're waiting for you outside, chico. You're not gonna last a fucking day out there," Dominic warned as they dragged him out. Brecee was frozen in place and couldn't even feel the oozing blood on his leg.

"Get up," the Asian guy ordered, extending a tattooed-hand. Brecee took it and allowed him to hoist him up.

"Thank you," Brecee whimpered. The medical staff rushed in and placed Brecee on a stretcher.

Fuck. He's looking for me. He's really gonna kill me.

"Dad, please that hurts," Brecee cried as he sat with his leg propped up. Despite being stabbed with a toothbrush, Dominic still managed to dig it deep enough into Brecee's leg to affect him walking. Brecee was surrounded by all of Steven's closest friends, including the one who saved him.

"This here is Donghae," Steven said as he pointed at the short man behind him. Donghae had a poker face but forced a friendly smile. He had scars all over his neck and shoulders that had turned a dark brown over the years.

"Just glad you're okay. Your dad is a friend of ours so we gotta protect his kid."

"Speaking of which," Ryeo broke in as he pulled a chair out. "Donghae said the leech mentioned something about the outside not being safe for your kid. What's up with that?"

Steven and Brecee exchanged nervous glances.

"I worked for Fredricko," Brecee said softly. "But I gave his name to the detectives. That's how I got time off."

There was a hush amongst the men. It was an unspoken rule not to give names.

"Fuck it," Donghae said with a shrug. "You know how many boundaries that fucker crossed? How many deals I lost out on? All his people are bound to rat him out. Especially after that shit he pulled on Steven."

As soon as the words left Donghae's mouth a look a regret flashed across his face.

"What are you talking about?" Brecee asked. Steven exhaled and turned towards Brecee.

"I really didn't want to involve you in this shit, son," Steven said sourly. "But I worked with him. Very briefly."

"What? But you acted like y'all barely talked?"

"It was a cross deal type of thing," Ryeo chimed in. "Everyone knew your dad was the shit."

"And once he realized he wasn't about to be on my level and make the same money, he needed me off the streets."

It started to sink in for Brecee. The way Fredricko took an unusual interest in Brecee from the very beginning.

He used me. He knew who my fucking dad was.

"Pops, I'm sorry, I—"

Steven hugged Brecee.

"Stop that. You ain't do shit. It's good you got his name to them cops. He's on the run now and is gonna keep running until they find his ass."

"And in the meantime, he'll keep sending in his coke-hungry pawns to do his dirty work," Ryeo said.

"He almost killed me," Brecee said quietly as he peered down at his wounded leg that was wrapped in thick bandages.

"But he didn't. Which means from now on, you gotta have protection," Steven urged.

"I saw that toothbrush shit he had. I can easily make one."

"Hell, no!" Steven croaked. "If them guards catch you with a weapon, they'll throw you in solitary and bump up your sentence."

"Your dad's right, Brecee," Donghae added. "Guards reward those who play by the rules. Let us take care of the hefty shit."

Brecee hated feeling out of control but he knew they were right. The last thing he needed was to worry about his safety.

"Ryeo, you tell the Young brothers to watch Brecee in C-block. Then Donghae, you got him in his class. I can cover him with Reggie and the boys in community," Steven ordered. It was like they were in the army and Brecee was the prized possession the enemy clans wanted.

Brecee respected his dad's need to protect and felt more at ease. The walls within the prison were no longer bland and lifeless. It was exactly like the streets where people were ruthless and blinded by their hateful ambitions.

New York was covered in snow after a blistering heat wave. The cops were constantly sweeping the streets after the last drug bust, so most dealing had to be completely underground in bar basements or secluded woods.

Fredricko had grown tired of the new order. He loved the lifestyle of the gaudy and shameless. He loved the way people would scamper away when he'd enter restaurants or look at him with awe. Now, he was nothing but a has-been dealer who had been lowered to the standard of hide-out.

His plan had been to escape to Mexico until things cleared up, however his name was continuously brought up and remained a major key to the mystery. Fredricko despised Brecee, not because he ratted him out, but because he was in the care of Steven Monroe and it would be harder to kill him.

"Sir, it's your nephew," Fredricko's maid said as she handed him the phone.

"Dom? How did it go?"

There was a long pause followed by Dominic's ragged breath.

"I missed, tio."

Fredricko kicked the lamp near him over and threw a vase at his huge mirror that took up an entire wall. The glass shattered and fell to the marble floors in large shards.

"How the fuck did you do that?"

"Tio, he's got watchers. That Steven dude has the whole prison against you," Dominic whined on the line. "Also, I heard from the guy next to me that Brecee knows about you and his poppa."

"Of course, he does. Of course he'd tell his son everything," Fredricko groaned.

"Tio, will you get me out?"

"I told you I would if you did your part. You're on your own now."

Fredricko hung the phone up and threw it across the room. Time was running out for him and his options were limited.

It never crossed Fredricko's mind that the kid he tried to use would find a way to turn him in.

"I was good to that little shit," Fredricko muttered to himself. Since the trial, all of Fredricko's places had been raided. He lost millions of dollars just covering his ass and keeping people quiet.

Steven Monroe was supposed to be the reason Fredricko died a rich man. The day he got Steven arrested was golden and everything fell into place. However, the irony was that it was the low-life son of Monroe that reaped the benefits of seeing Fredricko fall.

The back door opened and Satim, Fredricko's trusted right-hand man, came into the room covered in snow. He noticed the broken lamp and mirror and sat beside Fredricko.

"You have got to keep your cool."

"Dominic failed," Fredricko groaned.

"Of course, he did. I told you that was a dumb plan. I don't know why you listened to your coke-head nephew."

Fredricko glared at Satim. "I listened because my options were limited, you idiot."

"The only thing you need to worry about is staying out of the light. Brecee has a year sentence. He's gonna be out before you know it. If you wanna strike, strike then. Build your money back up and prepare yourself until then."

Fredricko closed his eyes and fell back into the couch. He pictured a bullet passing right between Brecee's eyes that night he was arrested.

"Can't believe I missed. I never fucking miss."

Satim lit a cigarette and took a long puff then handed it to Fredricko.

"Just be cool, boss. Everything will happen in due time," Satim promised with a sly smile.

CHAPTER SEVENTEEN

B recee's first eight months in prison whipped by faster than he expected. With the added protection of his dad's people and his days spent working towards his degree, he only had time to focus on himself. When Brecee wasn't in class he had long talks with Steven where they'd talk about life and love. Brecee mentioned Naudia and his heartbreak on losing out on her, and Steven reminded him of his lost love with his Ma. They bonded over their similarities and pains. It was as if they truly were the same person.

"Pops, do you think I'll get a second chance with Naudia?" Brecee asked out of the blue. He went on and on about how he knew Naudia had been too good for him at the moment, but there was still a part of him that yearned to be back with her.

"Son, no matter how good I think you are, the outside folks are different. Especially that Vontane girl."

"Naudia. Her name is Naudia. She don't like going by her parents' name."

"Those her parents, though, and unlike you, she's got a straight ticket into her daddy's business," Steven said with an exasperated sigh. "Your Ma worked her ass off at that hospital, but it still wasn't gonna get you to a high status."

Steven cocked his head to the side and jabbed his finger into Brecee's chest.

"So, I'll never get her back," Brecee said.

"No, son. I don't think you will." The realization wasn't brand new. It wasn't something Brecee hadn't recognized. But just like when he came to terms with losing Ma and Jordan, he was coming to terms that Naudia really was gone.

"Then I guess I'll be single for the rest of my life."

"If you got that attitude, then yeah," Steven chuckled. "Look, no woman wants a man who can't hold his own. All that 'I ain't shit' and 'things ain' never gonna get better' was too much to put on that poor girl. She was an angel for sticking around and I believe she loved you, but even the most patient, kindest souls got a limit."

Brecee could think of all the times he poured his frustrations on Naudia and she never cared to tell him to stop. She'd just hold him and run her fingers over his head until she slept. Then she'd kiss him in his sleep to make sure he stayed relaxed.

"It's just hard to accept it," Brecee admitted.

"You don't have to accept it now. But take it from me, if you use all this time in this shit to try and get your girl back, and she ends up not wanting your punk-ass back, then what? Focus on that degree and make something of yourself."

He was right. Life was hard in the outside when Brecee was hopping from job to job.

Brecee stretched his arms and legs out and leaned against the bench. It was finally warm again outside and the sun was blaring down on Brecee and Steven.

"Shit, this sun ain't no joke today," Steven whined. "Let's go back in before church starts." The prison ministry was a new venture for Steven and Brecee in the last three months. Even though Brecee tried to stay away from religion, it gave him a sense of peace.

The pastor, Hayden Kirkland, was also an ex-convict himself. He was a tall white man with badly drawn tattoos and a huge, red beard. His shoulders were broad and his legs sturdy, but the years after being in the street likely resulted in his beer belly. He claimed to have found Jesus after the death of his brother.

"He looked down into my soul and found the tiny bits of good left," he recalled. Brecee felt a tingle in his own chest when Hayden recalled the story. After Brecee's arrest, he fell into ultimate despair and the only things he could feel vividly was anger and hatred. Thankfully, his dad lessened it. The mention of Naudia

made that hole open up even more as the hurt settled in so deep, it stung worse than Brecee's stab wound.

"I'ma stay a lil longer. I'll catch you in a few, pops."

Steven waved and walked back inside. Brecee checked around him to make sure no one was in earshot, then leaned forward and closed his eyes with his hands pressed together.

"God, it's me, Brecee," he started the way Hayden instructed him. "I'm lost. I'm hurting real bad. I wanna thank you again for letting my sentence go by pretty smooth. I could've spent the rest of my days here. I also wanna thank you for keeping Ma and Jordan safe. I'm praying today to ask for clarity on Naudia. If she's really gone and out of my life, please let me just move on. I don't wanna hurt no more. I don't wanna keep chasing after her once I'm on the outside again. I wanna be free. For real this time."

Brecee opened his eyes and felt the warmth of the sun beating into him. The heat felt like a gentle touch against his cheek, as if God was reaching down and calming him. It reached into his chest and replaced his pain with hope. Brecee imagined God coming down from the sky and sitting next to him with his golden hand intertwined in Brecee's. The hope restored faith in his body. Not just for the sake of getting Naudia but to maybe one day love again.

A tear slipped down Brecee's cheek that was quickly swept away by a rough wind. It rattled the fence and shutters on the windows before calming down again.

"Yeah, I hear you. I'll leave it to you from now on," Brecee promised. He kissed his prayer hands, then stood and walked inside.

I'll love you always, Naudia. Ma. Jordan. But God has released me finally. I'm free for real now.

"Name, please?"

"Jordan Monroe," Jordan told the woman behind the front desk. She had a bad dye job and was smacking carelessly on a huge wad of green gum. The waiting area was blistering hot with a few flies buzzing around. There were faint cries from irritable babies and yells in the distant.

"You know it's not his usual visiting day, right?"

"I wasn't made aware there was a schedule. Anyways, I talked to the head guy last Tuesday and he told me I can see him any time since Brecee has gotten good behavior marks."

The woman rolled her eyes and typed furiously on the computer. After an excruciating minute, she leaned forward and gave Jordan a toothy smile.

"Doors open. Walk all the way down until you see the big red arrow."

Jordan left swiftly. He had exactly an hour. He promised Ma he wasn't seeing Brecee, just dropping off Brecee's usual care package. Ma had been too devastated about Brecee's sentence, so she had cut him out of her life completely.

Jordan was positive things would change once he got back out. Over the course of the last year, Jordan tried everything to busy himself and not think of his baby brother. It was impossible, though. Everything reminded him of Brecee, whether it was music or buildings he'd pass on the way to work.

An officer guided Jordan to a talking station towards the end.

"He's been called. Just wait here."

Jordan set the basket he had on the tiny desk space. It was full of commissary items like soap, tissue, shower shoes, deodorant. Ma made one special every month. The prison didn't allow her to send in food, so she made sure to stock his account with money to never go hungry.

"He's still my baby," she'd say as she wrapped the basket up. Jordan was warmed by her efforts. No matter how much pain she felt she'd never truly abandon her son. She just didn't want Brecee to know that.

"If he thinks I'm out here caring for him, he'll slip right back into being stupid and thinking he can always get out of shit."

Jordan was positive that Brecee would have a brand-new perspective on things, though. From what he heard, Brecee was a week away from his degree and had really good behavior. For the first time in many years, Jordan was actually proud of him.

There was a light knock on the window. Jordan looked up and saw Brecee beaming back at him. He was slightly thinner, and his hair had outgrown into a small fro, but he had a light behind his eyes that Jordan never saw before. Jordan picked up the phone with shaky hands.

"Little bro."

"Jordan."

"You look good, surprisingly."

Brecee busted out into laughter as he wiped his eyes.

"Nigga, they stay on my ass in here. But so do you. I'm shocked you came in this time," Brecee said with raised eyebrows.

"Well, I guess it would've been helpful to come in earlier instead a month before you get out. But it was too much for Ma and me," Jordan said with a wince.

"You don't have to explain it. I get it. You were under no obligation."

"Damn. Who is this wise, calm man I'm speaking to?" Jordan croaked.

"It changed me, bro. All the pain and disappointment. Pops taught me to channel it into something positive." Jordan shifted uncomfortably. Brecee could see his lips twisted into the usual scornful pout he did when he heard something he didn't like.

"So, you've been talking with Steven. How is he?"

"Dad. He's our dad. And he's good, actually. I don't think I would've survived this shit if it weren't for him."

"Did he ask about Ma?"

"Of course. But not in the way you'd think. He's on some real philosophical shit," Brecee laughed. Jordan nodded stiffly and squeezed his hands together.

"That's what I'd expect from seventeen years."

Brecee and Jordan stared at one another as angry thoughts passed through both of their heads. Jordan didn't hate Steven as much as Brecee did when he was younger; he tolerated him. He was like a stranger that had no effect on Jordan's life. For as long as Jordan could remember he carried the household on his back and picked up three jobs in high school to make ends meet.

He wasn't the type to complain, though. He preferred to carry his pain silently, a gift he was curious if Brecee finally picked up.

"So, are you going to be angry about being in prison?"

"What are you talking about?"

"I mean are you going to use it as a crutch for why you can't do certain things?"

Brecee steadied his breathing to hold himself back from saying anything bad.

"I get you only know me from when I was out there. All those years where I didn't do shit for myself," Brecee said slowly. "But being in here opened my eyes to so much. I'm sorry Jordan for putting all that responsibility on you and acting so immature. I've learned so much and really have changed. I hope you can see that for the better."

Jordan smiled, this time genuinely.

"I look forward to seeing that progress put to work."

Brecee was sure that Jordan had his doubts. As much as it infuriated him, he couldn't blame Jordan. All those years where Jordan had to cover his ass just to make sure things stayed afloat. Brecee never took into account how hard that was on his brother. He only saw Jordan as a hard-ass with a chip on his shoulder, who thought he was better than everyrone. Yet, it was Jordan who took the plunge to see Brecee in prison, not Ma.

Steven taught Brecee how to guide himself through his emotions when things got difficult. When people said slick things. Brecee had actually passed the test with Jordan of all people.

The next month, Brecee would be on the outside with the ability to walk freely and hold his head up. He didn't know what was waiting on him, but he was ready.

"Alright, Brecee Monroe. Your sample came out clean, so that's good," Terrie Rochell, Brecee's parole officer, said as she scribbled notes in Brecee's file. It was just past ten a.m. and Brecee was having his monthly visit to the parole office to ensure he was keeping up his end. It was a grueling process that kept him alert 24/7 but he was thankful to be making any kind of progress.

Brecee nervously twiddled his thumbs and sat upright in the wooden chair. Terrie noticed Brecee's stiff posture and chuckled, closing the file.

"Relax, Brecee. You're doing good. How's work coming?"

"It's...work," Brecee replied as he thought of the warehouse where he loaded boxes for ten hours straight. "I'm lucky a place even hired me."

The job hunt was vicious. Even though Brecee had an associate degree and great marks from prison, most jobs weren't too interested in hiring a convicted felon. After fifteen job rejections, Brecee eventually found the Nalleyville warehouse that shipped car parts all over the country. It was a dull job with older men who most likely had their run -ins with the law, and the place constantly smelled like old socks and burning rubber.

"The unfortunate reality for most that just get out of prison. But if you can keep a job for a year and prove you've truly changed as a person in the face of the law, then you'll find better positions," Terrie said with her pen pointed at Brecee.

"One that pays a lot better, too," he mumbled. "Only thing I can afford is to pay my half of rent."

Steven's great aunt Bertha Deb was the only living relative willing to house Brecee after he got out of prison. He was expecting Jordan or Ma to make decent arrangements, but they were radio silent when he got out. What was supposed to be a happy day turned out to be bleak, where the reality of the outside settled in. All his hard work and safety net was swiped clean because in the face of the real world, no one cares if you did well in prison. The simple fact of having a felony is enough to exclude you from the world.

Bertha Deb was eighty-six and blind in her left eye. She lived in Staten Island in a broken down, creaky home that moaned every time the wind hit it. Her refrigerator constantly leaked and there was a god-awful stench of mothballs. In Brecee's case, he had no room to be picky. She offered him the attic – a tiny space with a gaping hole in the wall that suffered an occasional leak. There were usually cockroaches and mice. Brecee couldn't tell if it was better or worse than prison.

His dreams of going into law were halted. Now he was actually working at a warehouse, barely making enough money and only had time to sleep and work. Life was dreary, especially without his dad by his side to give him wisdom.

"Brecee?" Terrie said, snapping him out of his pity party. "You should be proud. Most folks don't last a month, let alone two months back in the real world. You're doing really good."

"Except my Ma and brother haven't seen me sense. It's feels like it's been forever," Brecee snapped.

"Give them time. It's not just the prison sentence that's hard. It's their reputation that suffers, too."

"Fuck that," Brecee yelled loudly. "I'm their blood. I'm a part of their family. I know I haven't done great things but shit. What if I died? What if that punk actually took me out when I got stabbed? That's not family."

Terrie set her pen down and stared back at Brecee with sympathy in her large eyes.

"I know how you feel, Brecee. I was in your position when I first got out. It takes time and patience."

Hot, angry tears slipped down Brecee's cheeks, but he wiped them away quickly.

"I don't want no one to think I'm just sitting here being ungrateful. I've come a long way. I ain't complaining about working hard," Brecee said as he wiped his face. Terrie reached over and softly touched Brecee's clenched fist.

"It's okay to complain when things are hard on you. Just don't stop when it's hard. Keep going."

Brecee made his way back to the graveyard neighborhood Bertha Deb lived in. As usual, when he opened the door he was hit with the pungency of spoiled food and sweat. Bertha Deb was sprawled out on the rotting couch with her ancient cat purring in her lap. Her large chest heaved in and out slowly followed by a bear-like snore.

"Hi, Aunt Bertha," Brecee mumbled as he went to the refrigerator. There was an old casserole, the likely culprit of the nauseating stench, and day rice from the Chinese restaurant around the corner. Brecee reluctantly grabbed the rice to eat. His only task was to make sure Bertha Deb didn't slip or do something hazardous for her age. Despite being blind, she still managed to do alright as long as it didn't include cleaning.

Brecee helped around the house here and there but stopped after a while because she'd never notice a difference. According to his dad, she lost her sense of smell long ago. The arrangement to live with her was settled by his dad because he was the only one that knew Ma's house was a no-go.

"Pops, she made all these care packages for me. I think I'll be fine to go back."

"You're underestimating your Ma, boy. She's loving but she's still tough. She ain't letting you back in until you prove yourself worthy."

Brecee wished he could call his dad up and tell him how no one checked on him. No one cared to see how he was making it in the world he'd been out of for a year.

You were right, Pops. These folks don't care. I ain't proving shit to anyone but myself.

Brecee's only saving grace was the one phone call he got from his dad every week. Steven had used up all his phone

159

privileges making arrangements for Brecee, so he could only afford to hear Brecee's progress every Sunday.

"It's good, Pops, I'm really happy here," Brecee would lie. He always had the thought to tell his dad everything he was feeling. But it was no use. He didn't need him worrying. Instead, Brecee took up writing. He was never confident in writing his thoughts out, but he found a spare notebook in Bertha Deb's linen closet and started writing out every crazy thought. Some nights he felt so lonely he was sure he'd relapse or throw himself in the lake up the block.

The pain was unreal. The loneliness ate at his soul and made his thoughts heavy with despair. Even praying wasn't enough at times. He lived within the confines of rules, even on the outside. He felt like animal locked in a cage, never able to leave Staten Island except for his monthly parole meetings.

It ain't no life to live, Brecee wrote in the journal when he was on break at work. Lunch was the best time to write because he typically accumulated so many thoughts and poems in his head. He'd write until the buzzer sounded, then go right back into his work. He never talked to anyone or looked up from his work.

Why should he? The moment he entertained the idea of not wanting to be there he'd fall right back into his trap.

"You sure are a silent storm," a man next to him whispered. Brecee looked up from taping a box up to find Joey Merlot, a twenty-three-year-old with mousy brown hair and sea-green eyes, staring back at him with a mischievous grin. Brecee assumed he was the youngest worker there, but judging from the fresh shirt Joey had on, he had just been hired.

"Not much to say," Brecee mumbled back as he continued taping the box. He then hoisted the box onto the truck and started on another one.

"I'm Joey."

"I read your tag."

"And you're Brecee?"

Brecee stopped once more and looked him up and down. "Who's asking? Who wants to know?"

Memories of Dominic stabbing Brecee flashed through his head.

Can't trust none of these people.

"Well, damn. I was. I just got here, and nobody seems to be the talking kind."

Brecee's s face softened. He definitely had become uptight since he got out. It was hard not to be, though.

"Sorry. Just don't have time for fooling around," he said quickly. "Where you from?"

"Louisiana. You?"

"Manhattan."

Joey raised his eyebrows in shock. "Well, well. How the hell did you end up in Staten island?"

"Long story." Brecee's stories were shorter now. He no longer talked with excitement about life. There simply was none left.

"I got nothing but time. This truck going out and the next won't be here for an hour," Joey said as he loaded the last box on the truck. He had bruises and scars on his arms that trailed all the way to his stomach. Joey noticed Brecee staring and pulled his shirt back down over his stomach.

"What happened there?" Brecee asked intrigued.

"Long story," Joey said with a half-smile. "I got a sandwich and chips if you wanna share."

Brecee and Joey settled in the back of the warehouse that was littered with discarded metal and fast food bags. Joey handed a half of his sandwich to Brecee.

"No thanks."

"I saw that you didn't' eat. You gotta eat, man."

Brecee reluctantly took the piece and ate it hungrily. After the rice in Bertha Deb's refrigerator, he hadn't eaten much else. The sandwich was turkey with spicy mustard. It hit Brecee's taste buds and almost made him drool.

"I used to fight back in my neighborhood," Joey said with a mouthful of chips. "I used to get the shit beaten out of me."

"Why?"

"Not much else to do. My parents were barely there and when they were, they beat me, too. After I turned twenty-two, I made a promise that I'd leave and just travel around."

"And you ended up here?"

Joey laughed and bit into his half of the sandwich. "I got arrested here. I just decided to stay."

Brecee's heart started to pound. Joey was the first person on the outside he'd met who also had been arrested.

"Me too," Brecee said quietly. He could see Joey turn to gawk at him.

"Shut the fuck up. No way. You? You don't even talk!"

"You'd be surprised." It was a slight compliment that Joey couldn't see the felon in Brecee.

"What for?"

Brecee swallowed the rest of his sandwich and wiped his hands off.

"Drugs."

"Doing or selling?" Joey asked anxiously.

"Both. Mostly selling, though."

Joey's mouth gaped open. "That's so fucking dope, bro."

"Wait, what?"

"A real-life drug dealer?"

Brecee hit Joey on the shoulder roughly.

"Shut up. I ain't no drug dealer," Brecee whispered. "I said I used to. I don't do that shit anymore."

"But why? We barely get paid nine an hour here. You literally could be making what these fuckers make in a year in one night," Joey whined. Brecee had it. He grabbed Joey by the collar then pushed him back on the floor.

"That's the exact reason I got thrown into prison in the first place. Being stupid and thinking money will solve all my problems. Stop being such a kid," Brecee grumbled. Joey dusted himself off and started to walk away but he stopped.

"I ain't gonna be no truck loader all my life. Not when there's an easier way. Maybe you should consider that, bro."

Brecee watched Joey walk back into the warehouse as he was left with his fears.

Money. Freedom.

Having money would solve a lot of Brecee's problems. That familiar itch crawled up his leg and settled in his chest. He squeezed his hands together and breathed in and out several times.

There was no room for error, but the idea had already been planted.

CHAPTER EIGHTEEN

"**I** feel like I lost everything. My Ma, brother, and the only girl I ever loved. But this first year out taught me so much. It made me so much stronger. That's why I'm so proud to be working on things I'm actually passionate about," Brecee shared as he stood in the middle of a huge gym. He was in a circle of ex-convicts who were similar to him. They all had a past of drug use and dealing and fought to stay clean on the outside. Their prison sentences changed them, some for the worst, but eventually led them to understanding themselves better.

Brecee held up his favorite book, now with the front page missing. It was his bible in the darkest of nights and he felt proud to not just say he was a reader of books, but also a writer.

"After working at the warehouse last year, I discovered my love for writing. I wasn't the best at it, but I still loved it. I worked hard at it and decided to go ahead and publish my poems in my own book."

There was a resounding hum of praise as Brecee fought back tears. His book of poems was the only light he could find. It laid out every single fear and happiness he had kept stored inside. He reached into his pocket and pulled out a napkin. It was worn with small, blue flowers on it.

"I wrote on this napkin the day I was fighting on whether or not to go back into dealing," Brecee admitted slowly.

It had been the day after Joey encouraged Brecee to break back into dealing. His request was so small and aimless and Brecee could look right through Joey. He was an airhead, much like Brecee was, and did things that made sense in the moment. He chased after money that he would later blow on frivolous things. The burning came right after. It rammed into Brecee's veins, reminding him of how easy it was to get high.

There was a high from coke and dealing; the two things Brecee knew well. He was exasperated with the tug and pull of his life on the outside: Bertha Deb's rotting home, his barely livable wage, Ma and Jordan forgetting he existed. Where was the redemption in him breaking his back just to look like an outstanding citizen?

Pops was so wrong. It's not worth it.

That following day he missed work. He slept in his cold mattress, drenched in sweat, dreaming about snorting pounds of coke. He dreamed of the high he got from holding a gun in his hands and seeing people cower and respect him. Now, his boss just pushed him around and yelled demands. Where was the redemption in being reduced to a piece of shit again?

His body was crawling with angst. He needed it. Not a whole lot either; just enough to let him live. The sun was gone before he knew it and the night was pitch black with not one star in the sky.

Brecee rolled out of bed and hobbled down the squeaky stairs, through the new stench of day from Bertha Deb, and finally to the street. It had been so long since he detoxed and got clean, yet he could taste his old friend. The neighborhood was running with drug dealers and all he had to do was find one.

His body wouldn't even let him go to the torn down trap houses on the block, though. It pulled him to the only spot open a twelve a.m.: a rundown diner. The only people that came into the diner were lost souls. The music played washed up eighties music and there were only four lifeless waitresses who had soulless eyes.

"What you want?" an older waitress with saggy bags under her eyes asked. She looked like she hadn't' slept in years but still decided to throw on her raggedy, faded, pink work dress.

"Coffee," Brecee grunted. He couldn't drink. Smoke. Snort anything. He gripped onto the table. Just across from him was a wide-eyed little boy with a toy train. He stared Brecee down, noticing the cords sticking out of Brecee's neck as Brecee fought his urges.

He can tell I'm fading.

The waitress came back and slid the coffee on the table. She peered down at Brecee with those dead eyes with not one question or worry in them. In that neighborhood, it was nothing out of the ordinary to see people itching and sweating.

"Anything else?"

Brecee looked up at her, unable to stop the tears springing down his cheeks. He opened his mouth to say "nothing" but only a piercing sob came out.

"My Ma. My Pops. I want my parents," Brecee blubbered. He started to cry, hard. The waitress stayed put as her blank stare contorted to one of slight concern. The waitresses behind the counter also looked over, assuming Brecee was a new face with an old problem.

"I'll get Andy," the waitress muttered as she breezed away.

"Is that... your manager?" Brecee called as he wiped his eyes.

"Nah, local magician," a thin man with wiry, blond hair said. He had bird like features with a sharp, hooked nose and pointed chin. His teeth were long and jagged and his fingers pale with all type of puncture marks. He reached into his pocket and pulled out a small white bag then slid it to Brecee.

"On the house if you're looking for work. I don't recognize you," he said in a whisper.

"No, no, no. I don't deal no more," Brecee said as he pushed the baggie away.

"Anymore? Maybe you should. It's just how things are," Andy insisted. Brecee pushed the baggie away and kicked Andy from under the table.

"I said no! Get the fuck away from me—"

Andy punched Brecee right in the nose. Brecee held his nose as blood spurted onto the table.

"Idiot," Andy muttered as he got up from the table. The waitress placed a single paper napkin on the table with a wince.

"For your nose, sweets."

Brecee stared down at the napkin as numbness filled his body.

That's when the words started coming through. It was like a part of his head was pouring all these emotions out and couldn't stand to have them locked inside any longer. Brecee pulled his dull pencil out of his pocket and started writing.

Black skies mixed with paint

It rains, it stings, it cries

I'm a star without the 'straint

I reach, I run, I die.

Born under the heat of God

I was meant to sink

Ma tried to lend the rod

Pops sanity took the link.

Save me sun from this night

'Cause it's shining hard

That glimmering, powdery light

Let me live at least without guard

Brecee stared down at the napkin with a relief. It lifted the edge off of his shoulders as if his spirit could finally read what it was trying to communicate all those years.

He stuffed the napkin in his shirt and stood up on uneasy legs then walked out.

Andy stopped by him tugging on his elbow. "You'll be back."

Brecee pulled his arm away and pushed through the door without looking back. It was as if he was walking out of the cemetery and back into a life full of light. The walk back to Bertha Deb's was surreal. The sky was pitch black but Brecee was restored. He smiled in the dark and marveled at how his body still managed to carry on despite the pain.

"I was relentless," Brecee said as he had sat back down after reading the poem.

"We're so proud of you, Brecee. You're truly an inspiration," Terrie said with tears in her eyes. Terrie was the one who got Brecee to start attending the help group a year ago.

"Thank you, Terrie."

"So, what now?" a woman with short locs asked.

Brecee zipped his satchel bag up and put it over his shoulder.

"Well, it's Sunday. So I'm going to see my pops."

Sunday was their day. Brecee and Steven. They'd meet in visitation and talk for as long as they were allowed. Brecee sent his dad lots of money and care packages now that his poetry book was making good money.

The publisher was impressed with Brecee's background and writing ability. They found his voice to be unique and inspiring. After signing with them, Brecee went on a brief tour around the US where he talked to young juveniles, sharing his story. He made sure to send every postcard to his dad.

"Look at this here," Steven said with misty eyes as he stared down at Brecee's hard cover book. "My boy is published!"

"That's a special copy, too. Open it."

Steven carefully opened the first page and found a personalized message:

To the man who raised me without even knowing it. To the man that lifted me out of my darkest moment and showed me my own light. To the man who saw good in me when no one else would. To my mentor, my listener, my teacher, my pops.

Steven closed the book as tears fell from his eyes.

"I'm so proud of you, son. I wish I could be out there with you," Steven said with a sad smile.

"You will, Pops. I'm opening your case back up. You're getting a second chance."

"How? Don't waste time trying to find no expensive lawyer—"

"I'm gonna be your lawyer, Pops. I went ahead and enrolled in school again. I'm getting a full degree then going straight to law school. I'm not giving up. I'm gonna fight for you the same way you fought for me," Brecee promised. "You not about to live out your years in here."

"I believe in you. You got everting you need to do what you want. So, I'll trust your word."

"I love you, Pops."

"I love you, son."

Brecee left the prison with a heavy heart. But he was still determined. Seeing his dad always made him feel better which was why Sundays were his favorite. He still had one more stop, though.

Naudia stood in front of the board meeting in her best pumps and brand new suit. It was bought after she finally graduated. Her mother made plans to buy an outfit she thought would suit Naudia, but Naudia refused.

"I can make my own decisions," Naudia told her as she took off her cap and gown. It was supposed to be a cheerful day, but as usual, her thoughts drifted to Brecee. When she learned he was released and then later published a book, she couldn't believe her ears.

The local news had interviewed him to promote the book and she nearly fainted at the sight of him. He was no longer the fragile, child-like Brecee she'd fell in love with. Instead, he was a man. He stood strong and confident and spoke with clarity without the worry of his words not being understood.

Naudia wanted to tell him how proud she was. How she always knew he'd make something of himself. But time had changed them both. She promised her dad once graduation was over, she'd be in his office taking over the junior position. Despite her heart being heavy with the reminder of Brecee at every corner from huge posters and his books on the shelves, Naudia made the quiet decision to honor her freedom. Even without him.

The office didn't question her. They didn't size her up the way they used to a year ago. They listened. They jotted down notes. Naudia's mother would often gloat on how proud she was of her for "putting her worst year behind her." The only thing was Naudia would never hate Brecee. She was strong and confident because of the love they had.

She could only smile when she imagined Brecee living out his dream, finally and in the right way.

***

"That son of a bitch," Fredricko growled as he threw his plastic cup at the TV. A guard placed his hand on his waist belt and stepped forward.

"Don't push it or you'll be back in solitary."

Fredricko recoiled, his anger settling in his chest. After being on the run for several months, he eventually lost his reign to a

173

sneaky cop. It was such a small error on Fredricko's part that he dreamed of taking his life at every moment. How could he have been so dumb?

Right before he was to cross into Canada, he stopped at a pub. His supply of coke had run out and he wasn't thinking clearly. The beer was the only thing that would have calmed his heart. The cop disguised himself as a simple-minded drunk with an overgrown beard and slurred words.

They spoke gleefully for a few hours until Fredricko's inhibitions lowered enough for him to reveal the real reason he had to leave.

"Can you believe I've been in this shit all these years only to lose out to the son of my rival?" he said with beer spittle dripping down his chin.

The man looked up quickly with his eyes wide.

"Who's the rival?"

Fredricko laughed bitterly. "Fucking Steven Monroe."

"And his kid?"

"Brecee!"

The man rubbed his beard as the sympathy left his eyes. "Does that mean the guy on the TV?"

Fredricko stood up and bowed drunkenly. "At your service," he said with a chuckle. The man grinned and pulled a pair of cuffs out of his back pocket.

"You're under arrest for murder and drug position."

Fredricko gasped as the rest of the empty pub set their beers down and revealed cop badges. The man he trusted to be a simple-minded stranger ripped off his beard and forced Fredricko's hands behind his back. The world felt like it was going in circles as Fredricko was escorted to a cop car and reporters swarmed asking a million questions a minute.

"How did you know Brecee Monroe?"

"Is it true you murdered your partner?

"Why did you frame Steven Monroe?"

After a year in prison, the news of Brecee's success finally reached Fredricko. He tried to destroy every TV and inmates that spoke positively of him. The mention of Brecee being called anything but the rat he was made Fredricko full of rage.

However, he suffered through months of solitary confinement, tasers, and occasional stabbings that made him vulnerable and weak. As he sat with a permeant frown on his gaunt face, he knew he had officially lost to the one he was sure he aimed his gun at.

***

There was a knock on the front door.

"Jordan, hurry and answer it! I think it's Brecee!"

Jordan rushed to the door and swung it open. Before Brecee could even say hello, Jordan wrapped him in a big bear hug.

"Little bro!"

"Hey, Jordan."

Brecee pulled away and patted Jordan on the shoulder.

"Thanks for inviting me over, Jordan."

"You can drop the formalities, bro. You're home!"

Brecee winced at the sound of "home." He hadn't been back to Ma's house since before he was arrested. Ma and Jordan only reached out after his book was published.

"Brecee, baby!"

Ma ran over and hugged Brecee tightly. Brecee hugged her back as the nostalgia of her perfume made him feel like a little kid all over again. Jordan and Ma stood awkwardly looking at Brecee like he was a stranger.

Brecee was noticeably different. He'd started working out and grew his hair out so that it was long enough to hang by his ears. He stood taller and dressed simple but sharp with a dark blazer and jeans.

"You're all grown up," Ma said with a smile. Brecee could smell the sweet cornbread radiating from the kitchen.

"I'm also really hungry," he said.

"Let's eat!" Jordan called.

They all sat at the dinner table like a family. Jordan and Ma hammered Brecee with questions about his experiences in prison and the book tour.

"Did you meet scary people?"

"How was the food?"

"Do they pay you well?"

The questions were startling to Brecee. Even though time had passed, he was still wounded over Ma and Jordan not being there for him. Out of the corner of his eye, Brecee saw the drawer still full of letters. He stood up abruptly and walked over to it.

He pulled the drawer all the way open and gasped at all the letters. He ran his fingers over them.

"Can't believe they're still here," he said.

"Yeah, well I sure wasn't touching them. That buster is lucky I even kept them all these years."

"Buster?" Brecee repeated. Jordan sensed Brecee's intensity and laughed to try and ease the air.

"C'mon, Brecee. Even you wouldn't read them growing up."

"I was a kid then."

"You were damn near twenty-six, boy," Ma said with an eyeroll.

"Brecee. My name isn't boy," Brecee said with growing contempt. Ma turned to look at Brecee and shook her head in disbelief.

"I know your damn name. I named you, didn't I? I don't know why you acting all high and mighty over them damn letters."

"Because Pops was the one. He watched over me when I was in prison," Brecee said as he kept his hand over the letters.

"He also was the reason you were in there," Ma said with scorn.

"Ma, come on," Jordan muttered as he squeezed Ma's elbow. "Things are just different with Brecee.

Julie rolled her eyes and stood up from her chair with her nostrils flared.

"I don't see how things are different, though. That man left me with two kids because he was too busy chasing after money, when he was really just full of shit."

Brecee slammed his fist on the counter so hard that the dishes rattled. He raised his hand with his finger shaking and pointed at Julie.

"I'm not denying what you went through, Ma. I'm not saying you can't be angry, but for once in your life, please just let shit go. It's been years since you've talked to him. He's changed. I've changed. I just want you to be happy," Brecee said.

"You've changed cause you wrote a book? You made money? Only years can show that. Until then, dinner on Sundays is the furthest you'll get here."

Ma folded her arms against her chest and Jordan hung his head. Brecee locked eyes with Jordan in hopes he'd come to his rescue. Instead, Jordan kept his gaze lowered and adjusted his glasses.

"We're always happy to see you, little bro. You just gotta see things from our perspective," Jordan said weakly.

"Your perspective?" Brecee asked. "Is that really the only perspective that matters?"

Julie started to respond but stopped as she considered his comment. It was never her intention to hurt Brecee but she knew if she let go of the mistrust and welcomed him back into her life completely, it would shatter her for good if he couldn't keep her trust.

Brecee reached in the drawer and grabbed all of the letters until he had them in his arms. He walked to the door without a word and opened it.

Julie had every desire to pull Brecee back and whisper how sorry she was. But she had no idea how to soften the anger in her heart after the pain she had. It consumed her the point of no return.

"This the last you'll hear of me," Brecee announced with a crack in his voice. "I love you both."

Just like the shabby diner that Brecee escaped death, he once again escaped travesty with an armful of his father's letters. He took a bus back to his apartment in Soho and found peace once he closed the door shut. His apartment wasn't the extravagant one Fredricko had but it was just right for Brecee. It was a studio apartment with tall ceilings and brick walls.

Brecee decorated it with artwork and poetry and made sure to have a stash of his father's records. He sat on his couch and dropped all the letters by his feet. As he grabbed for one all he could think of was that look in his dad's eye when Brecee showed him his signed copy.

His smile and approval were the only things that mattered. Brecee took a deep breath and cut open the first letter. The future was unsure and Brecee had no idea how he'd be united with his dad again. But he had a life supply of letters that his dad poured his love into, and as Brecee sat on his vintage couch in the apartment he paid for with his hard earned money, there was nothing but gratitude and love in Brecee's heart.

ABOUT THE AUTHOR

J. Brinkley was born in Tifton, Georgia. He writes in the genre of urban fiction and urban romance. In 2019 he was awarded the urban book of the year award by the African Americans On The Move Book Club (AAMBC).

He fell in love with writing as a teen and decided to take up creative writing classes to hone his skills. He published his first book in 2015. He has self-published a dozen novels under his own company, Voma Publications. His stories center on memorable characters and timeless truths about humanity in all its glory and in all its ugly ruthlessness. His books are an embodiment of his unconventional philosophies about life and love through spellbinding stories that leave the readers wanting more. Stay alert because he has more amazing new stories for you all to get engulfed in. Learn more about author J. Brinkley at: www.authorjbrinkley.com/

or on Amazon: http://amazon.com/author/jbrinkley/

Join my email list for new book updates and freebies.

http://eepurl.com/g4sW0H/

Join my book group:

https://bit.ly/2yt7s1R/

Made in the USA
Monee, IL
22 December 2020

55351123R00111